POKERGEIST

Michael Phillip Cash

ISBN: 1512074969
ISBN 13: 9781512074963

To my Casella and Salzman clan:

Good times in Vegas + Friends like you = Amazing memories

"I used to be a heavy gambler. But now I just make mental bets. That's how I lost my mind."

—***Steve Allen***

Prologue

Like taking candy from a baby, Clutch Henderson thought. He took a deep pull on his whiskey, allowing the burn to numb him from gullet to stomach. The room reeked of smoke, even though it was not allowed in the main ballroom during the tournament. Overhead, giant television screens focused on two players. Clutch looked up, winked, and watched the camera close in on his craggy face. *I still got it.* He smirked at his image. He was tall, lanky, and deeply tanned, which accentuated his silver hair and light eyes. Even though he was pushing seventy, he knew the ladies still found him attractive. They didn't call him the Silver Fox for nothing. Clutch patted the blister pack of Viagra in the pocket of the polyester bowling shirt that he wore in homage to the Big Lebowski, the fictional kingpin legend. Gineva would be picking up a celebratory bottle of champagne right now, as soon as she clocked out at the Nugget. They wouldn't give her the day off today—the bastards. There was a good chance he was going to make an honest woman out of her tonight…a rich, honest woman.

Clutch shifted in his seat, his hemorrhoids making their presence known. They burned his ass more than the cocky kid sitting opposite him. He looked over to his opponent who was sunk low in his seat, his face swallowed by the gray hoodie he wore. Adam "the Ant" Antonowski, boy wonder, who rose from the ranks of online card games, had beaten out a seemingly impossible one hundred sixty-five thousand players to earn a coveted seat at the International Series of Poker. His pimply face peeked out from under oversized sunglasses. Clutch sneered contemptuously at him. *They let everybody play today.* The kid did look bug-eyed with those enormous glasses. Adam curled his hands protectively over his cards, his bitten-down fingernails repulsive.

"Rookie," Clutch muttered under his breath, his lips barely moving.

"Looks like Clutch Henderson is praying, folks," Kevin Franklyn said into his mike from where he sat in a small room watching the game. He was a former champion turned seasoned sportscaster on the poker circuit, well respected, and the senior of the two anchormen. He was completely bald, his fleshy nose slightly off center on his craggy face, a victim of his youthful and unsuccessful boxing career. He'd made a mint once he turned to poker and had never looked back.

Stu James shook his head. "Clutch could be at his last prayers; this kid is the terminator." Stu was a tall cowboy with wavy blond hair and mustache left over from his 1970s poker-playing heyday. He looked like a country singer.

"Let's see if Clutch can exterminate the Ant," Kevin replied.

They shared a laugh. The sportscasters wore matching light blue jackets with the Poker Channel logo on the chest.

Kevin nodded, placing his hand on his earbud, and said, "Yes, this is it, folks, in case you've just tuned in. A record fourteen thousand entrants, and it all comes down to this—the final moments. The rookie versus the pro: it could have been scripted by a screenwriter. David versus Goliath. Adam 'the Ant' Antonowski going up against the legendary Clutch Henderson."

Kevin continued, "Legendary, yes, but Clutch has yet to take home that million-dollar bracelet, Stu. This must be his eighteenth try at the title."

"Nineteenth. However, he did come in sixth place last year."

Kevin nodded. "But the Ant is certainly the Cinderella story of the year. An online poker phenom who beat out thousands of players in a twenty-dollar online satellite game. And here he is today. How old is he?"

Stu turned around to a huge monitor. "I'm not quite sure, but I found out a lot about him earlier today when I interviewed him. Let's take a look."

Stu was in a suite overlooking the Strip. It was hotter than hell outside, but the room was icy cold. The Ant slouched in a Louis XV Bergere chair, his hands deep in the pocket of the jersey hoodie. The gold brocade of the chair was a stark contrast to the varied shades of gray he habitually wore. His Converse-clad feet lay propped on a golden rococo coffee table. Stu noticed that Adam seemed unaware that the rubber of his tennis shoes was peeling off the gilt surface of the coffee table. Every time he moved, another strip of paint flaked away.

Stu leaned forward, his large hands gesturing the spacious suite. "Nice room, Ant." Everything about the newscaster was big, from his shoes to his huge chest. He was a former ranger-cum-football player and an avid golfer as well. The Ant truly resembled an insect next to the bigger man. "You have quite a view."

The Ant shrugged indifferently. "I don't care about stuff like this. I'm happy with a room in Motel 6."

"This is a far cry from Motel 6. Why do they call you the Ant?"

"I'm small," the Ant said. He smiled, revealing tiny, ferret-like teeth that looked mashed together. A frizzy curl escaped his hood to land over his shiny forehead. "But I can carry fifty times my weight in chips." He laughed.

"Ha!" Stu joined him. "Fifty times. Is that what you're expecting to take home?"

"Maybe more, if I can help it," the Ant added defensively.

"Adam—I mean, Ant—you're coming into the final table with little more than half the chips in play." Stu paused for effect. "What's your strategy in the face-off with the legendary Clutch Henderson?"

The Ant looked straight into the camera, his dark eyes fierce. "I want to eat that old shit alive." The curse was bleeped out by the station.

Stu shifted uncomfortably. "That's pretty competitive, son."

"Let's get this straight. I'm not your son, Stu." This was said with dripping scorn.

"All right, Ant." Stu's voice turned decidedly cool; he did not like this kid. The sportscaster was freezing as well. What the hell was wrong with the air conditioner? Stu suppressed a shiver as he smoothed his mustache. The Ant was cold as ice; not a drop of human kindness flowed in his veins. Not only that, but he could swear the kid's lips were turning blue. He wanted to end this farce and get out of Dodge. "So, how do you plan on winning against one of the greatest cash players of the last century?"

The Ant glanced out at the stark light in the picture windows. Heat shimmered in the desert, making the horizon look smeared and indistinct. The Strip was jammed already; a long line of red taillights filled the road as cars made their way down Las Vegas Boulevard.

The ants go marching one by one...Ant hummed the nursery song in his head, lost in the moment.

Stu pulled him back. "Ant?"

The younger man stared at him blankly, as if he'd just awakened. He twisted to look at the messy bar, just off camera. Crushed cans of beer and energy drinks littered the floor of the suite, and laundry was strewn all over the bedroom adjacent to the living area. Turning back slowly, dismissing one of the most important sports interviewers on television, the Ant said brusquely, "Next question."

"All right." Stu pursed his lips, trying not to lose patience. *Maybe the kid is on something,* he thought. He'd been playing in eighteen-hour shifts for days now, beating out thousands of players. The interview was going to the crapper fast, and this surly guy might be the next world champion. *Give me something.* He checked his notes and then blurted, "How does it feel to rise from relative obscurity and find yourself face-to-face with the one and only Clutch Henderson?"

"Look, this story is about me, right?" The Ant jabbed his finger into Stu's face. "Not him. I'm the greatest player. I'm gonna create my own legacy, and it's gonna be tonight."

Stu sat back in his seat, shocked by the Ant's hostility. "Isn't that a little premature articulation?" Stu couldn't help the jab. This kid was nuts. He must be wired on the cans of caffeinated drinks tossed all over the floor of the bar area.

The screen faded as the two sportscasters turned to face each other.

"Interesting interview, Stu. So, what did you really learn about Adam 'the Ant' Antonowski?" Kevin chuckled as he shook his bald head with amusement.

"Not a whole lot, Kev. He is a close-mouthed little guy." Stu turned to gaze down at the single table where ten million dollars in cash had been strewn across the green baize in anticipation of the winner. A chunky gold bracelet glittered from the nest of cash, looking like pirate plunder. "It's so quiet down there, you can actually hear the Ant thinking, *I am the best player at this table.*"

Kevin rolled a pen between his fingers. He looked at the camera and continued with his commentary. "The fairy-tale story versus the legend. Let's not forget that Clutch may be the greatest earner in the history of the game: fifty million in lifetime earnings, one hundred twenty-one cashes, twelve final tables, and four number-one best-selling books."

"What about his instructional videos? He made a mint with those in the nineties. Looks like the Ant's asked for a break.Getting back to Clutch, he wrote what many call the Bible of Poker: *Clutch Time: To Live and Die at the Poker Table*. Will he make history tonight, Kevin?"

"He should. Been trained by the best—poker runs in the family." They shared a laugh.

"I'd call the Hendersons poker royalty."

Kevin nodded in agreement. "I'll say. Clutch is well-respected on the circuits; not many of those kind of guys left. He's a true gentleman, a dying breed. I sat down and spoke with him earlier today. Let's take a look." Kevin turned back to the screen.

"You're close," Kevin grinned at Clutch. Clutch inclined his head with a gracious smile. They were in his residence, a ranch in the seedier part of Vegas. Clutch sat on a gold velvet sofa covered with plastic slipcovers in a heavy Mediterranean style left over from the seventies. His girlfriend, Ginny, beamed from the kitchen as the interview progressed. Just past fifty, she was a chubby Filipina with brassy blond hair that clashed with her olive complexion. Kevin knew they'd been together for more than ten years, even though Clutch was still married to his wife, Jenny Henderson. Kevin paused for a minute and wondered if Clutch ever accidentally called Ginny Jenny or Jenny Ginny. That could make for some uncomfortable moments.

Ginny leaned against the doorjamb as the spotlight shined on Clutch's silver head. She had pressed his shirt earlier today and made the sharp crease in his pants as well. His scuffed cowboy boots were too old to take the polish, and only she knew that cardboard replaced the worn soles.

"Very close," Kevin pressed. "One play away from claiming your first-ever International Series Main Event bracelet."

Clutch looked happy; his blue eyes were dreamy. "Livin' the dream, man." The camera caressed his face.

"How do you feel?"

Clutch cocked his head. "With my fingers," Clutch said, wiggling his slender fingers for the camera. He glanced to Ginny as if to share a private joke. Winking, he smiled widely and a blush rose across her ample chest. She had great tits, Ginny did. Clutch knew that for a fact. He'd paid for them. He turned back to the interviewer. "Look, I've been playing this game since my granddaddy showed me the difference between an ace and a deuce. I've prepared my whole life. I've been taught by the best."

"Buster Henderson practically created poker."

"You ain't lying," Clutch agreed. "We didn't have a kitchen table. We ate off a poker baize, and there was always a game going on. Ruthie, my grandmother, was a pretty good player too."

"Yet it skipped a generation."

"My daddy died on the beach in Normandy," Clutch explained. "He never had time to learn the game."

"And your mother?"

"Never knew her. Buster and Ruthie raised me. They lived and breathed poker."

"Must have been an interesting childhood living with not only one, but two poker legends."

"Yeah," Clutch agreed darkly. "It was a barrel of laughs."

"What do you think Buster would say to you if he were here today, as you enter the final table?"

"'Better not screw this one up, boy, or I'm gonna kill you.'"

They shared a chuckle. "He was certainly a character," Kevin added.

"Yep." Clutch wasn't smiling anymore. "A real character."

"All kidding aside, even if you lose, second place has a hefty payout." Kevin looked at his notes. "You stand to win four million."

Clutch shook his head. "Sometimes it ain't about the money. My grandpa won that bracelet over sixty years ago. It's time for me to win mine."

"Hmmm. Clutch, how do you feel about the advent of online players today—namely, your final opponent, the Ant?"

Clutch sat forward, his hands together, his face thoughtful. "The Internet has more porn than you can shake a stick at. What good is that? You can't touch a computer. It's sterile. In the end, the game ain't real if it's through a machine. Romance and cards have got to be in real time, face-to-face." He let the comparisons sink in. "Nothing like the feel of a real woman."

"Hilarious, Clutch." Kevin laughed, sharing the macho moment with him.

"Now the real world has real women." Clutch glanced back at Ginny, who grinned back at him. She had the worst teeth. They'd never fixed her teeth in the Philippines when she was a child. That was the first thing he was going to do when he won, take her to have implants. Well, after he got a new car, paid his bookies, and paid off his back child support. She never asked for anything, Ginny. She was a good woman. "Poker is a game about communication. It's about reading people, knowing what they are thinking. You can't communicate over the Internet. You can't have a relationship with a keyboard and a screen—well, at least not an honest one. You can't learn poker with a machine. Ain't natural."

"Have you got any old tricks up your sleeve?"

Clutch looked at the frayed fabric of his dress shirt. The stripes were so old that there was just a hint of color in the thin cotton. He looked at the gray hairs sticking out of the cuff. He touched the bony point of his wrist, imagining the heavy weight of the bracelet. His grandpa had left *his* bracelet to Clutch's cousin, Alf, who had never even played poker. Clutch had wanted it for so long—every year scraping the money together to get into the tournament, playing with infants, hacks, and women who thought they could flirt him out of the game. He was good. He knew he was the best, and he should've won a hundred times. He shook his head. *A thousand times.* It came so close, so very close, only to escape his clutches.

"Clutch…" Kevin's insistent voice interrupted his wandering mind, pulling him back. "Clutch, you were saying?"

"Oh, we gonna teach that lil' doggy how to make pee pee on a wee-wee pad." The screen faded to black.

Kevin's shoulders shook with laughter. He turned to Stu. "That Clutch—he is something else."

"I'll say. I think he has his metaphors confused. He may need a can of Raid instead of a wee-wee pad. Oh, the Ant is back from his break. Let's see how the game is going."

Clutch and the Ant sat opposite each other, the room tense and silent. The older man pressed his cards into the table, bending just the tip to glance at the letters or numbers in the corner. *Kings, a good solid hand.* He kept his face impassive, stifling a yawn. The Ant simply ignored him, a bored expression on his face. Between them, a colorful cascade of chips littered the table. The room crackled with excitement. Clutch looked up at the dealer, who stonily stared into space. He smiled, and the dealer turned and nodded respectfully, revealing perfect teeth against his dark skin. They both looked to the Ant, who bristled with hostility.

Clutch narrowed his eyes, and a trickle of sweat began to make its way down from his temple. He stared hard at the Ant, whose dark glasses made him an enigma. The Ant was looking everywhere except at him. Why wasn't the kid studying him, looking for tells, the signs that hint at what he is holding? He watched his opponent intently. The Ant glanced upward before he made a move, as if asking permission from the atmosphere. While he couldn't see the kid's eyes because of the dark glasses, Clutch knew he was looking toward the ceiling from the tilt of his head. A few times, Clutch caught his own eyes gazing in the same direction, wondering what the punk was up to. The room became hot. He was willing to take this to the mats. Based on the kid's whitened fingertips, Clutch's gut told him the younger man had nothing. Clutch had a decent hand. He peered at the Ant's cards on the table, as if he could see through the design to the faces hidden underneath. The kid liked to bluff; he had watched him do it all through the tourney. Clutch was willing to bet his last chip that the Ant had a junk hand. "Check," Clutch said quietly.

"No check, old man. I bet three million." The Ant pushed five stacks into the middle of the table. The crowd hummed with excitement. The Ant pulled off his glasses to glare hard at Clutch, his mouth pulled tight with intensity. Clutch looked into the younger man's eyes and saw nothing. Nothing.

Clutch shrugged. "You wannabes sure think you know how this game is played. Lemme tell you something, partner…" He placed his Stetson on his head as if to make a point.

"Spare me the sage advice, Cowpoke. You're done. I'm waiting to stick a fork in you."

"Eight million," Clutch said, his voice serious. The crowd applauded loudly as he pushed in a huge pile of chips.

"I just started, Pops, and you want to go down in flames already. Raise! All in," the Ant sneered.

Clutch waited. He had patience. A murmur echoed through the room. He could swear he heard the ticking of a clock. He wanted to draw out the moment. His heart started to pound in his chest, pulsing so hard he felt it all the way to his toes. "Call," he said so quietly that the dealer leaned forward to confirm.

The Ant dramatically turned over his cards, revealing an ace and a seven, both of them hearts. The red cards reflected back at Clutch until they filled his vision.

A slow smile spread across Clutch's impassive face. He watched the younger man, savoring the glory as he slowly flipped his cards, revealing pocket kings. He had two kings—a good hand. Not unbeatable, but the kid had nothing but an overcard.

"Here comes the flop," Clutch said aloud as he watched the dealer place the ace of spades and Clutch's own heart sank in his chest. Now the Ant had a higher hand: two aces. The crowd's gasp turned into a roar as the dealer spread the next two cards on the baize, revealing a king of hearts and deuce of hearts. He'd dodged a bullet; his three kings would beat the Ant's two aces. Clutch took off his cowboy hat; the sweatband was soaked. His silver hair lay plastered against his head, the imprint of his hat looking like he had worn a vise. "Trip cowboys, pissant." Clutch drew out the last word into a hiss.

On the table were two hearts. Two cards were yet to be revealed: the Turn, and then the River. Sixty-forty in Clutch's favor, he estimated. Clutch felt his heart quiver with uncertainty.

The kid had a draw, two cards to go, and all Clutch needed to do was avoid a heart that did not match the table to claim his prize. The crowd exploded. The Ant stared at the card on the table, his expression hostile.

"We don't need a commentary, old man. I got eyes. I can see," the Ant snapped. The Ant's dark eyes glazed over for a minute; he looked away and then turned back, his attention restored.

Clutch sat back in his chair, suddenly tired. His shoulders ached, and he longed to be back home in bed watching television. But the bracelet. He was so close. He glanced at the Ant's cards and then studied his own. The patterns swam before his tired eyes as though they were alive. He was there, almost there. He could feel the heavy weight of the bracelet on his skinny wrist…the cash in his empty pocket. Sweat dotted the Ant's upper lip, and his eye twitched. There were so many chips spread across the table that the pot seemed obscene.

The Ant half rose from his seat, his face eager. His dark eyes glowed hotly, with red pinpoints in the pupils. He looked demented. His fingers pressed whitely against the green baize of the table. All he needed was another heart, and there were two cards left to go.

The Ant stood completely; Clutch was surprised at how short he was. He would barely reach Clutch's shoulder. "Great hand, Pops," the Ant nodded sarcastically. "But you need *heart* to play this game."

The dealer barely breathed as he waited for the right moment to deal the next card, the Turn.

The crowd stood together as if on cue, the babble of thousands of voices drowning out the pulse in Clutch's head. His body thrummed, and his face grew as red as the cards, sweat drenching his shirt so that it was plastered against his tense body. Feeling his collar choke him, Clutch undid the top button of his shirt. Suddently it occurred to him that he might come in second. It would be a nice purse, four million at least. But after taxes and the funds to pay off the loan sharks, he'd barely have enough for his kid or Ginny's teeth. Truth was, he didn't give a shit about the dough—he wanted the bracelet. He needed that trophy to wear on his wrist for the rest of his miserable life. Too bad Buster wasn't alive to see it. He wanted to shove it in his face and gloat. It sparkled from its spot on the table. Clutch swallowed convulsively, his neck feeling tight. He looked at the creep across the table. The Ant didn't deserve it; Clutch did. This was the closest he'd ever come. He stared at the bracelet, the gold at the end of the rainbow. He could hear his grandfather's voice, dead these last forty-five years, saying, "It's about the game, stupid. Not the gold. You play like crap. You never listen to me, boy." *Yeah,* Clutch sneered, *easy for you to say. You won a bracelet in 1954*. Clutch glanced down at his two cards, his kings. With the third on the table, he had three kings, a good hand. He had to piss…really bad.

The dealer turned over a six of clubs. The audience moaned. A black card, not a heart. Without the fifth heart, the kid would bust. Clutch's breath stilled in his chest. He was almost there. His heart pounded in his chest as if it were a kettledrum. One last card to go. He looked at the insect's hand. The kid's hands were trembling, his knuckles bony white like a skeleton. He had nothing. This was it. He had this. The dealer paused, his hand hovering over the deck. His manicured fingers caressed the top card, and then he flipped it onto the green table. An eight of hearts lay on the baize, earning the Ant a winning flush. The crowd buzzed, a thousand voices washing over Clutch's numb face. His breath left him in a slow deflation until he felt flat. He wanted to disappear.

The Ant yelled like a little girl, his hands high up in the air. He pranced in front of the bleachers to the screaming fans and then mugged the camera. Kevin raced from his spot, mike in hand, to the older man. "Clutch! Clutch! What happened? That was so fast."

Clutch stared at the cards, his face impassive, the pain of his broken heart heavy in his chest. "I…I…" Words failed him. He couldn't breathe. The room was stifling, closing in on him. His vision narrowed to the cluster of cards on the table and the bracelet winking at him. They shimmered before him; the noise of the spectators was muffled. His ears rang. He still had to pee. In fact, he was drowning. He heard laughter. It was familiar. He looked around frantically to see who was laughing at him. The pain started in his chest and radiated to his shoulders, clamping around his jawline. His eyes dimmed.

He felt Kevin's chubby hand grip his shoulder. It hurt. The announcer's voice came from far away. "Clutch… Clutch, are you OK?"

No, he wanted to scream, but his own voice seemed foreign, the words coming out jumbled and thick. *No, my dream died.* He watched the room recede, the world strangely quiet, as the floor came up to meet his chin.

The Ant turned to see the older man fall. *Oh,* he thought as he heard Clutch's head connect with the floor. *That's gotta hurt.* He turned to his adoring fans and pumped his fist into the air, the bracelet gripped in his clenched hand.

Kevin struggled to get down on his knees. "Clutch… Clutch." He shook the old man's shoulder. His face drained of color. "Get an ambulance," he screamed. He looked closely at Clutch. "Help…" he said sadly, knowing it was too late for an ambulance. They needed a hearse.

CHAPTER ONE

One Year Later

A gray haze hung over the Bellagio poker room, the thick air muffled with the sound of murmuring voices. Telly Martin leaned his face glumly into his palm, trying hard to control his expression. His dark hair needed a haircut, but that cost money, so he was going for a shaggy look, he told Gretchen. The longer hair complemented his high cheekbones and indigo eyes. He was trim—just a bit on the thinner side, he knew. He was watching, he'd told his mother a week ago. Watching his small change, he added to himself. There just wasn't enough right now—the money only went so far. He'd bought into this game an hour ago. It was a cheap game, low limit, but that was about all he had left in his budget this week. He refused to take any more money from Gretchen, that was for sure. If this one didn't pan out, he'd rethink the cab driver job Gretchen had suggested again last week. He didn't want to do that, though. It would interfere with his games. Cab drivers put in long hours, had to be available for the events that went on all the time in Vegas, and he'd miss his chance to play in the International Series. All he had to do was come up with the ten grand. *Ten grand.* Telly sighed. *Not much three years ago, and today an impossible dream.* He had a good job in IT at one of the casinos. Worked the computers in the communications department. It was boring but steady. He'd bought a nice house, Gretchen had moved in, and he had planned to marry her that spring. Then the casino had been bought. The purchaser had an existing IT department. Telly was redundant, they'd told him. He didn't feel redundant—*irrelevant, maybe; redundant, definitely not,* he thought hotly. He was one of a kind, he knew. He was the only one in the department who always brought in doughnuts on Tuesday. How could that be viewed as redundant? Didn't he organize the yearly softball game that raised money for the Children's Cancer Society? Who was doing that now? he wanted to know. He had created the Seniors Glee Club, arranging for a local nursing home to have entertainers from the casino's show come and sing with the residents. That program was laying an egg, he'd heard. They didn't have anyone on staff to keep up with it. But Telly was redundant, unnecessary, and currently unemployed.

"Today, Telly," Hamdi, the dealer, formerly from Cairo (or so his nametag informed them), pointed to the cards in the middle of the baize. "It's your bet, *sur.*" His hometown accent drew out the vowels, confirming his Egyptian heritage.

Telly looked up at Hamdi, smiling. "Like it here, Hamdi?" Playing at the casino was nothing like a home game. There was no repartee, and socializing was frowned upon. He thought being a professional poker player would be…well…more fun. It wasn't. The tables were tense, with a distinctly unfriendly feel. While Telly was a reasonable player with his weekend buddies, he was mortified at how little he really knew. One fumble and everybody lost respect for you at the table. The trouble was, nobody had patience.

"Indeed." Hamdi smiled, a mouthful of white teeth, and added, "You are holding up the game. Your bet."

"Um…" Telly looked at the sea of faces around him. They were in varying degrees of openly hostile to bored out of their minds. "Four dollars?"

"Are you asking, *sir*?"

The man to Telly's right smirked. "I reraised. Weren't you watching?"

"So," Telly stared at the sparse pile of chips in the center, "I'm supposed to…" He looked at his cards again. His mind had gone blank; he didn't remember exactly where he was in the game. He dragged a hand through his dark hair. *That's what you get for daydreaming.* He hated this feeling.

Hamdi leaned closer. "If you want to see his hand, you have to bet another four dollars—bring it to a total of eight."

Telly looked at his meager stack of chips. He'd double his money if he won. He stared at the ceiling. Then he considered the revolving plastic image of Marilyn Monroe, her dress fluttering around her, spinning at a kiosk of slot machines across the floor. *Gretchen would look pretty in that dress,* he thought absently. His ears picked out a chorus of cries celebrating a slot win. He failed to see his neighbor observing his every move, the unlit cigar frozen in the other man's mouth, the smell of wet tobacco offensive. Telly gingerly picked up eight dollar chips, sliding them into the pile. "Call." He liked the way he sounded. Like he was a professional. Really. He'd tell Gretch all about it tonight when she got off from work. They turned over the rest of their cards.

"Two pair, fives and tens," Hamdi informed the table, sweeping Telly's coins away toward the gruff older man next to him.

"Well, I had two pair too," Telly flushed, explaining his error as he watched his chips join the other man's stacks.

"Sugar," the woman next to him said, "he had two tens showing since Third Street. You had sixes and fours." She had long turquoise fingernails with rings on every finger. She stroked her stack of dollar coins suggestively. Telly turned to face her, noticing that she wore thick fake lashes that sort of resembled the roach he'd killed this morning in the apartment. She sported an artificial beauty mark above her top lip. Her hair was long and black, with odd bangs cut straight across her forehead. It was a hairstyle for a young person, Telly thought, observing her. It was like playing with a wrinkled Angelina Jolie. The woman looked hard at him, the sequins on her cowboy jacket sparkling under the muted light. Tiny lines radiated from her thin lips, and the dark red lipstick bled into them. She looked like a zombie spokesperson for Revlon.

"How could I have missed that?" He looked back at the older man, still sucking on his cigar.

"You a virgin or something, sugar?"

"I beg your pardon?" Telly was aghast.

The players at the table laughed. There were a few snorts mixed with chuckles.

"You're new at this game is all I'm saying." She fluttered the roach eyelashes. Telly was fascinated. She had a line of rhinestones pasted to each eyelid.

"I've played my share of games," Telly said defensively.

"A regular Clutch Henderson. Listen, buddy, if you're playing in the International Series next week, let me know. I want to sit right next to you," an older player wearing a hearing aid said from across the table.

"Me too." This from a retired African American postman who now played nightly at the casino.

Telly gathered up the remainder of his chips, his face flush with embarrassment. "I'm glad I provided you all with an evening's entertainment," he mumbled. He looked around the table at their wizened faces. Most had skin so tough it looked like his old baseball mitt buried in the closet at home. Half of them smoked, the other half drank, and who knew what the hell the zombie woman did in her spare time. *Did he really want to do this?*

"Sorry if I interrupted the flow of the game," he apologized.

"A word of advice," Cigar Chomper called out in a grizzled voice.

"Yes?" Telly paused expectantly, touched that the man would help him out.

The old guy cleared his throat, the table stilled, and he sang, "You got to know when to hold 'em, know when to fold 'em..." The table erupted in glee at his rendition of the Kenny Rogers classic, and even Telly chuckled, laughing at both them and himself.

"Oh, right, thanks a lot." He stuffed the chips into his pocket and waved farewell, smiling sheepishly. "I'll keep that in mind. Good night." He heard the raucous laughter even after he left the poker room to walk through the enormous casino to cash out at the cashier. The floor's busy pattern danced before his tired eyes, and he continued, head down, feeling just on the edge of stupid. Maybe he should look into driving a cab, until he landed a better job, instead of pursuing this pipe dream. It was just that the videos made it seem so easy...anybody could do it. He was tired of working in an office for the same paycheck every week. While he had invested only a couple of weeks in this enterprise, he had won at the Station Casino last Tuesday. They had dined out on his winnings for at least a week, as well as paid the rent, bought shoes, and wired money for the electric. The problem was, the money didn't last long enough. He had to leave enough of a stake for the next game, and when he lost, the one after that. *I could make it work if I hit a streak,* Telly thought. After being let go from his job, he'd held onto the house as long as he could, but without a steady income, he missed a few of the mortgage payments. The bank had put it on the market last week. He and Gretchen had moved into a weekly rental in a part of town that had more pawn shops than grocery stores.

Telly felt his arm being pulled. He turned to find his friend Misty gripping him. "Telly, I called and called you. You didn't answer. Is everything OK?" She was just past twenty-five, slender and tall, with a perky blond ponytail. A tray of cigars and cigarettes hung from a strap over her capable shoulders. He banged into it gently, but they both grunted.

"Sorry, Misty," Telly said.

"No worries, Tel. How'd you do?"

He shook his head. "Nah. The cards were against me."

Misty looked at him sympathetically, her eyes soft. "Don't you worry, Telly. You're going to hit it big. I know it."

Telly shrugged, his face turned downward.

"Anyways, I wanted to thank you for the signed Pete Rose baseball card. Gregory loved it."

"Did the surgery go well?"

Misty swallowed, her gray eyes filling. She lifted her shoulder. "We're hoping they got it all. He starts treatment Thursday."

"I'm glad he liked it. It was one of my favorites. My grandma bought it for me."

"Aww, Telly. You're so generous. How about you and Gretchen come by for a barbeque next week."

Telly thought for a minute. "I'd love to, but the Series starts and I'm hoping to make the entry fee."

Misty rested her hand on his shoulder. She leaned forward, kissing his smooth cheek. "Then I'm planning on watching you on the television when you finish in first place. Don't give up!" Misty was momentarily diverted by someone asking for a package of smokes. Telly waved and walked toward the valet. He considered spending the last of his stash on a ten-dollar ice-cream cone. He stared at the dripping fountains of chocolate, his mouth watering. Telly saw the line and then decided to keep his change for something both he and Gretchen could enjoy. Moving on, he passed the atrium, the fragrance of hundreds of flowers heavy on the air. He heard waterfalls, birds chirping. Even though he was inside a giant casino, he felt like he was strolling in a park. His feet slowed at the window of the jeweler just before the lobby of the hotel. In the center of the display, a radiant-cut yellow diamond rotated on a circular bed of white velvet. Set in platinum, with two dazzling baguettes on either side, the buttery-colored stone glowed warmly. Telly stood transfixed by its beauty. His eyes focused on the rainbow depths of the diamond, and he pictured it on Gretchen's hand. She had hocked the ring he bought her last year when he needed dental work done.

"Like it?" the clerk asked. She was so thin that you could almost see through her. Slicked-back red hair that could not have been produced by nature was scraped into a painful bun. She minced outside in dagger black heels. "I asked if you like yellow diamond," she said in a thick Russian accent.

"It's really nice."

"Nice!" she laughed. "'Nice,' he says." Telly stared at her enormous teeth. "You buy for your girl. I make you good deal."

"How much is it?" Telly asked boldly.

"Eighty thousand dollars, if you pay cash." She said thousand pronouncing the *th* with a *t* sound.

"When I win the Series, I'll be back for it," he told her.

"When you win the Series? Ya, I wait for you." She threw back her head, laughing lustily.

CHAPTER TWO

Clutch wandered down the Strip. Night had fallen, and it was showtime. The Strip was like a parade, cars inching along, the cacophony of hundreds of varieties of music blaring in the sultry night air. He stood before the Venetian, watching rowdy young men screaming from the balcony. They held yardsticks, a beverage in a thirty-six-inch plastic container colored in sherbet shades acting as camouflage for the intense alcohol content. Honking car horns, laughter from various groups of people, and the babble of different languages filled the night air. Clutch paused, leaning on the railing of a fence, the oversized bronze sculpted heads of Siegfried and Roy behind him. A group of girls, one wearing a cheap rhinestone tiara with a short white veil, banged into him, squeezing him into the shrubbery to take a picture with the statue. They were happy, silly with drink, their dresses too short, their hair too high, their eyes too shiny. Clutch perked up. *Women,* he thought. One of the things he missed most from this world—a close third after whiskey and poker. And Ginny, of course, he added guiltily. He admired the tight dress, the maid of honor's backside stretched her fabric so tightly, he swore he could see…Clutch reached out to caress her curves.

"Hey," one of them smacked her friend on the shoulder. "You poked me."

"No, I didn't," the bride of Frankenstein shot back. Her hair was piled high on her head and the tacky veil hung lopsided in her ditch-water blond hair. She was weaving, her heels getting stuck in the cracks of the sidewalk.

"Stop," one of the more sober ones added. "I told you not to wear those shoes, Brittney."

"She keeps banging into me. Your purse is goosing my ass."

Brittney spun on her friend, holding her impossibly small purse in the air. "How can this little thing affect your big ass, Tiffany?"

"What did you say about my ass?" Tiffany stalked over to Brittney. A breeze ruffled her hair, and she stopped to shiver as goose bumps pebbled her skin. She felt like she'd walked into a cloud. The night was so dry, yet she felt chilled, her skin damp with dew. "I'm cold."

"You're shit-faced. Let's take a selfie and head back to the room," a third girl chimed in, holding up her phone.

The girls all laughed and crouched low, their heads together like a bouquet, for a picture. Clutch hovered above them, trying to get into the shot.

"Lemme see." Tiffany grabbed the phone. "What's that? Stop touching my ass, Brittney!" She spun wildly in an off-kilter circle.

"What? I'm over here. Cut it out, Tiff. No more Jell-O shots for you! Hey, what happened to our picture?"

The three heads looked down at the phone. "What's that?"

"It must be a reflection from the light," Brittney reasoned. A large orb hovered before their faces in the picture, slightly obscuring their images. "Wanna do it over?"

"I think I don't feel too good." Tiffany gagged, gagged again, and retched violently into the bushes, Siegfried and Roy silent observers to her agony. The girls patted her back, and then, hooking their arms under her shoulders, they headed off toward the hotel.

"Let's grab a cab?" Tiffany offered.

"I'm out of money. And I don't feel so well either," Brittney responded, her face green in the weak light.

"The evening air will do you good. We'll walk until we can't walk anymore." They all laughed, weaving as they pushed on farther down the Strip.

Clutch looked down at his vomit-covered shoes. *That's what you get for messing with the living,* he thought ruefully. He could almost hear his grandpa say, "You stupid idiot; you touch shit, you gonna smell." Clutch shook his feet and then strolled the Strip. He headed toward the Bellagio Fountains. He had nowhere else to go. People walked around him, through him, as if he weren't there. Well, technically he wasn't. He was there, but not there. Oh, he saw the light that everybody talks about, but he had no urgency to leave. It pulled at him, but he resisted. He wasn't ready to go, he told a white-haired guy in an iridescent suit and enormous feathered wings. The fella was always hovering, just out of his eyesight. Sometimes it annoyed him, and he would try to ditch him. He thought back to that day right after he collapsed. He felt himself being lifted, high outside his body. He floated next to that colorless winged guy, watching in a detached manner. Wait, he couldn't believe it. His daughter was in the crowd, watching, her eyes wide with horror. He hadn't even known she was there. Hell, they hadn't talked for over a year. He passed her, ruffling the hair on her dark head, and then meandered around the poker room, waiting there, watching the Ant get his check. His eyes caressed the bracelet, even as it was clamped around Adam's thin wrist. He floated back to Ginny and watched her place his ashes on the table next to the television. She really mourned him, Ginny. He wished he had told her he loved her, at least once.

His second-place winnings were in limbo, just like him. Jenny, his ex, and Ginny were battling it out in court. He'd never had a will—there never seemed to be a need. Now it looked like only the lawyers were going to get anything.

He was at Ginny's the day the goons came about a week after he died. They burst into the house, breaking the door, grabbing Ginny by the shoulders. They were thugs. One was short with tattoos covering his entire neck, going up his bald head. The other was so fat, he practically waddled. With a baseball bat in one hand, he knocked off her knickknacks from a small table.

"Where's the money?" the tattooed one demanded.

"What money?" Ginny cried. "Who are you?" she asked, but she had a gut feeling she knew who they worked for.

Clutch moved forward but found himself held in place by unseen hands. He kicked, used his elbows, but it was as if he were suspended in midair, entangled in an invisible web.

"Clutch's winnings. They say he won four and a half million at the game," the short man told her in Spanish.

"I didn't get anything. It's not mine to get."

"What do you mean?" he demanded.

The first thug was walking around, opening drawers, looking in the closets. He picked up the bronze urn that held Clutch's cremains. He lifted the finial, opening the lid.

"Stop," Ginny begged. "Please, it's all I have left of him."

"Where's the money, bitch?" The fat one slapped her across the face. Clutch fought with the invisible manacles holding him, listening to Ginny's moans.

"I told you, it's not here. His wife…he was still married. His wife is inheriting the money, or maybe his…I don't know. All I know is that I'm not getting a dime."

"Where does the wife live?" he asked as he walked over to the trash. Ginny shrugged.

Clutch felt lightheaded. A buzz started from behind his forehead to travel down, making his inside hum. He watched the man hold the jar of his ashes over the garbage.

"Noooo!" Ginny screamed. "Please, if I get anything I'll give it to you. I don't want anything but Clutch."

"Where does the wife live?" he demanded.

"I don't know, I told you."

Dots swam before Clutch's eyes as his ashes floated in a graceful arc from the urn to the garbage.

"I always said Clutch Henderson was trash."

Ginny was punched once in the face. A white business card fluttered onto the floor next to her foot.

"Expect to be contacted. My boss, Victor, will be wanting to speak to you. You," he said as he pointed to her, his eyes serious. "Be ready for his call."

Ginny clutched her cheek, her mascara running down her face like a macabre clown.

What could the loan shark have to say to me? she wondered. She couldn't pay Clutch's debts; she barely had enough to pay her own bills. She hoped they wouldn't bother Ruby; she worried her bottom lip. The kid had enough on her head, what with rehab and her crazy mother.

The door slammed behind her. Ginny slid to her knees crying as she crawled to the scatter of ashes on the floor next to the waste bin. With bloody hands she swept them into a pile. Her tooth lay whitely in the middle of the mess.

CHAPTER THREE

Telly stood outside the Bellagio, the soaring music matching the movement of the fountains. Spouts of water shot up with each rich note sang by Andrea Bocelli, and he wondered, too, if it was indeed time for him to say good-bye. He was miserable at this game. He was always the top player at his weekly game with his buddies and had played online with pretty good results. Yet, somehow in the casino, he felt like the country mouse among the city mice. All his moves, his experience, left his head. They intimidated him with their private poker language. No matter how much he looked it up and studied the verbiage, he always missed the one they used at the table that night. Telly was shy, and sometimes the aggressive behavior stunned him. He had to admit, though, it excited him too. Sitting with the grizzled group of hard-drinking, tough-talking poker players was thrilling. However much he loved the atmosphere, he couldn't read the other players. Gretchen had said he should get it out of his system, but that was almost a month ago. She wasn't so generous about the idea anymore. Something was bothering her, and that worried Telly. The poker playing was so different from what he was used to. When Telly sat at the table, he tried not to feel like the skinny kid with nerd glasses, the one all the other kids pushed around. It was mysterious. If he squinted just right, they couldn't tell he was so new he could barely contain his excitement when he hit a hand. The Bellagio was cool, the fountains were cool, and saying you were a professional poker player was cool. Telly had wanted to be cool his whole life. There was some indefinable thing about certain people that made them cool. The way they answered, the swagger, the clothing they wore. No matter how much Telly tried, he never had the cool factor, except for when he sat at a poker table. Or so he thought, until tonight. The wizened lady poker player tweaked his ego. She saw through him, and soon so did the others. Who was he fooling?—he was a computer nerd who was trying to take a step out of his boring box to live a dream. It wasn't as though he'd quit his job, he'd told Gretchen. He'd sent out his résumé and gone on interviews, but his heart wasn't in it. He wanted more. This was his chance to break the mold his parents had cast for him when he was still in high school. They had mapped out his life before he had a chance to leave the cocoon of their household. He was never given choices. He was the smart one; he had to pick something steady. He had to shoulder the responsibility for his bipolar brother. He had to grow up fast and not look back.

Telly leaned against the fence, admiring the graceful water. He tapped his foot in time to the song about a chorus line. The water moved synchronized, so perfectly—it was a marvel of technology. He analyzed the patterns, working out the equations that made them work. He knew every button that was pressed, every line of programming it took to make the water dance. It was predictable—boring, like him. He felt himself pushed hard from behind. Three giggling girls, clearly drunk, surrounded him, and the bride of the trio draped herself onto Telly.

"How 'bout a lil' kiss," she puckered her overfilled lips for a smooch.

Telly disengaged her arms with a smile. "Much as I'd like to accommodate you, I'm engaged to be engaged."

"What stays in Vegas stays in Vegas." Brittney pushed her bridal veil so it hung drunkenly off the ponytail that now dropped to one side crookedly.

"What *happens* in Vegas stays in Vegas, stupid," Tiffany said. She pushed Brittney on her tattooed shoulder. "Don't you know the commercial?" Tiffany wrapped her arms around Telly, her hands caressing his face, dislodging his glasses. "I think we are gonna have to go home with you, 'cause we don't have no more money."

Telly grabbed his glasses before they could fall and hastily put them back on. "Do you need a cab?"

"We're out of money, honey, but we got plenty of time." The bride rested her sweaty head against Telly's jacket, pushing Tiffany out of the way.

Telly dug deep into his pocket, finding a few crumpled dollars. He took Brittney's hand, leading them up the small incline toward the cab line. The other two girls followed him like sheep.

"How you doin', Telly?" Clarence the doorman asked as he tipped his hat.

"Where are you staying?" Telly asked, turning to the less inebriated one.

"Excal...Excalbit...Excalibra," the girl struggled, her eyes rolling. No help there.

"I don't feel well again," Brittney moaned.

"Clarence." Telly handed the doorman a dollar. Clarence shook his head.

"This one's on me, Tel. Thanks for saving my hard drive."

"I'd like to hard drive you." Tiffany pulled Telly's face, kissing him hotly on the lips, shoving Brittney behind her.

The cab pulled up, and the cabby leaned over, smiling. "Where to?"

"Take them to the Excalibur. How much?"

"Gonna be at least fourteen."

Telly pulled out a crushed twenty from his pocket. "Get them back safely."

"What's your name?" Brittney asked. She draped herself on his other side, so he was sandwiched between the two girls.

"Telly."

"Don't you want to be with me tonight, Telly?" She twined her fingers in his long hair. "It's my last night as a single girl," Brittney whined, drool collecting at the corner of her mouth.

"Much as I appreciate your kind offer, I'd rather remember this night with the memory of what it might have been."

"Oh, Telly," Brittney sighed, and then she threw up all over his legs.

He helped them into the cab, waving as it pulled away. The Bellagio cleaning crew was already soaping up the cobbled pavement.

"You need another cab, Tel?"

"Nah." Telly shook his head. That twenty was his stake for a game tomorrow. He was done, finito, kaput. Back to the grind. First thing tomorrow, he'd have to start looking for a job. He'd tried and failed. It was time to return to reality. *It's time for daydreaming to go back where it came from—your head,* he thought ruefully.

Clutch stopped to observe Telly escorting the inebriated group of girls to a cab. He knew that guy, had seen him at the table. He was what Grandpappy would call a Donk, or Donkey, a lousy player. In fact, it was what Buster had first called Clutch when he started teaching him poker. It still rankled, hearing that term. He would hit him over the back of his head every time he made a poor move. He'd clutched the cards so tightly to keep them from falling out of his hand, the name changed from Donk to Clutch and stuck. Nobody knew that tidbit of trivia, and Clutch was grateful that it remained a secret that his trademark, respected moniker, had started out as a derogatory term of disgust from his grandfather. Clutch winced and muttered, "Rot in hell, you old bastard."

Telly walked down the hill, the fountains dancing, a new song playing. Shoulders slumped with resignation, hands deep in his pockets, he glanced down at the speckles of vomit on his pants, feeling embarrassed. *Just my kind of luck,* he thought, his face reddening. It seemed to be the story of his life right now. He was sick of the whole thing.

He loved poker, yet even this didn't feel like fun. The sneering condescension of the other players changed the dynamics, making him both unwelcome as well as uncomfortable. So what? Let's say he was a new player, he reasoned. Why couldn't they respect his willingness to learn? Instead they looked for a reason to ridicule him, poke fun at his expense. *What's wrong with people today?* he mused.

The hot Vegas winds blew warm air around him. He looked across at the theater marquee. Legendary performers filled the screens. He watched the tall showgirls in their red-feathered headdresses walk daintily down a long white staircase with their heads held high. He knew what it took to be a dancer; Gretchen had trained for years, but a car accident in high school had ruined her knee, killing her career. She was never bitter about it, his Gretchen—sweet, charming Gretchen, the most likable person he'd ever met. She was so beautiful, he could stare at her face for hours. Gretchen was the type of person who always found the good in people. When he lost everything, she quietly packed up the house, found the crummy weekly rental, and never complained. He could be having the worst day, but when he walked in that door, her grin washed away his despair.

The ex–Playboy Bunny filled the screen with her long loop to wrangle sheep. Telly fought the disappointment biting at the back of his throat. Why did some people make it while others languished undiscovered and unfulfilled? Gretchen had put together a show too. She was prettier than the playgirl, and even if singing was not her forte, she could be charming and funny. She'd auditioned it all over Vegas, but even the third-rate casinos didn't bite. He wished they'd bought Gretchen's show, but they hadn't. The vagaries of life teased and tormented them. Careful, he told himself, you are sliding down that slope into bitterness. Taking a deep breath, Telly resolved to find the peace that Gretchen brought him. The screen changed, and now that medium from Long Island who talked to dead people lit up the night. Her face revolved, showing her two-toned black-and-white hairdo and obsidian eyes. She had a warm personality; he liked her show. He waited to see the show times, hoping he and Gretchen might be able to catch one night of the limited engagement. If anyone could lift his spirits, it would be Georgia Oaken. Seriously, though, even if watching her connect with supposed spirits of the dead from the other side would be entertaining, he doubted she could change his derailed life.

All of that was in his hands, however incompetent he was. He certainly felt incapable of correcting his life's downward spiral. He couldn't understand what had happened. He was the one who finished school, got a good job, paid his taxes, and carried out every responsibility laid on his young shoulders. He anticipated everyone's needs, did his due diligence, and performed his duties with pride. He never expected to be kicked out of the club. It was as though he had the plague now. Once he was let go, none of his colleagues wanted to associate with him. It was as though they were afraid his bad fortune was contagious. He didn't get it—he'd avoided all the pitfalls of adolescence, not succumbing to the temptations that had destroyed his friends' lives. He'd played by the rules, and then the rules had punished him. Telly had fallen through the looking glass where the world was reversed, and all his good deeds rewarded him nothing; all his planning and work was a waste of time. He was in an alternate state, where he was unglued from all that was familiar in his former reality. Here, his education worked against him; his work ethic meant nothing; and his morality was useless. The yawning hole of depression sucked him to its precipice. He forced himself to breathe; he didn't want to be like his brother, Manny. Telly told himself to stop; he was feeling redundant again.

He pushed his hands deeper into his pockets and felt the hard surface of a coin. It was a penny. That was it, his last penny. He laughed ironically. A chill danced up his spine, and a cool current of air enveloped him.

Raising the coin, he considered Abraham Lincoln's face. Honest Abe. Honest Telly. What had being honest ever done for him? *Between you and me, Abe, being honest didn't work out too well for you either.*

He flipped the coin high so that it spiraled in the air above him. "I just want to win something. Anything. I don't want to be a loser anymore."

The music muted, and all Clutch heard were Telly's mumbled words. Telly's wish intruded into his thoughts. He looked at the dude's vomit-covered shoes and then glanced balefully at his own. He felt something for this loser, as if Brittney's vomit connected them in some way.

Clutch watched the coin fly and then reached out to grab the penny in midair. The wish crystallized in the air, creating an electrical current between them. Clutch's heart expanded. He didn't want to be a loser either. They were attached by more than just vomit, he realized with a smile. He pushed the coin to fly high and wide, arcing over the tall shooting water. "Truth is, I want one more shot at the bracelet!" he shouted.

Telly watched as the penny hung suspended for a moment and then started to fall back toward him. He was such a loser, he couldn't even throw a coin for crap. For one gravity-defying moment, it hung suspended in midair, and then it shot out over the fountain as if propelled by a rocket. The coin spiraled down, landing with a loud *plop* in the water, ripples flowing outward in widening circles. He stood transfixed, watching the spiraling circles on the mirror-like surface of the pond. As if on cue, the fountains sprang to life, Sinatra's voice filling the thick evening and advising those assembled to start spreading the news.

The white-haired man in the iridescent suit hung over the water, glorious wings flapping behind him. He watched Clutch intently.

"Are you sure that's what you want?" the angel's melodious voice questioned.

"Why are you following me? Who are you?" Clutch sneered.

"You know who I am, Clutch. I know you've figured it out," the angel's voice echoed.

Clutch laughed. "I never expected you, that's for sure. The devil, maybe, but certainly not the likes of you."

"No such thing as the devil, Clutch."

"So you say. What's your name?"

"Sten. But you knew that, didn't you. We were introduced when you crossed over."

Clutch nodded absently. It was still hazy to him. "I remember a bit," Clutch said.

The penny appeared in the angel's long fingers. He expertly fiddled it through his fingertips, much like a professional gambler would.

"You're pretty good at that," Clutch said with admiration.

"I'm pretty good at a lot of things. And so are you, Clutch."

Clutch shook his head ruefully. "Don't think so."

"What's it going to take for you to realize that you are?" The angel glowed a little brighter.

Clutch narrowed his eyes and said, "You sound like a teacher. I don't like teachers. I was never good in school."

Sten hovered for a minute and then settled on the railing. "Why are you still here, Clutch? What do you really want?"

"All I ever wanted was to win that bracelet," replied Clutch.

Sten shook his head. "Be careful what you wish for…" He tossed the coin toward Clutch, who deftly caught it, surprise on his face. "There's your change, Clutch. Don't blow it."

The air shimmered and he was gone. So was Telly.

CHAPTER FOUR

Telly walked the mile and a half to the small apartment he shared with Gretchen. They had rented it soon after he'd lost the four-bedroom house. He had tried to keep it, but really, he was underwater with it anyway; foreclosure was the only way out. He had bought the home during the building boom in the early part of the millennium—houses springing up overnight, prices escalating. He'd purchased the trilevel home at the height, knowing he was overpaying, but with his promotion coming up soon he was confident he could afford the big mortgage. He never expected the casino to sell and eliminate his position. He had banked on his security. It was a sure thing—his field was important to the casinos. He had looked for work, but nobody was hiring at his former salary. He'd lowered his requirements, but wherever he interviewed, he was overqualified. They were afraid to hire him at a low salary, figuring he would move on as soon as something better showed up...only nothing better ever turned up. The interviews got scarcer and scarcer. Telly did a stint at a bank, and then he consulted on a few projects and ended up never getting paid. Companies went belly-up before they could pay him. It was after the last fiasco that Gretchen had urged him to follow his dream and try to become a professional poker player.

"It's now or never," Gretchen told him in bed one night. She leaned over, a long, ash-blond curl playfully tickling his cheek. She was worried about him; he was sinking into a depression. *A man can only take so much rejection,* she thought, biting her bottom lip. Telly was so smart; he just needed a boost to his confidence. She would do anything to make him feel better.

"Nah, Gretch. It's not steady. I have to get us out of this place." Telly turned to take her in his arms.

"Listen. You let me try that belly-dancing thing."

"You were so good at it." Telly kissed her small upturned nose. She had the creamy complexion of a blonde with large blue eyes. She was so pretty, she took his breath away every time he looked at her. Telly couldn't believe his good fortune when she had agreed to date him, much less marry him. Gretchen was sweet, kind, and beautiful. He adored her.

Gretchen shrugged a shoulder, the white strap of her gown sliding off. "Well, nobody liked it enough to buy the show." Her eyes were downcast; Telly knew they were shiny with tears. "It's this bum knee of mine; it ruins everything."

Telly caressed her knee and then squeezed the kneecap gently, making Gretchen squeal with delight. "You're the bee's knees," he said. He bent down to kiss them. Then he pulled her close and whispered, "I think you are the most beautiful girl in the world."

"You aren't so bad yourself," she giggled, kissing him back.

"I wish I could have made your dream come true, but booking a belly-dancing dog act was a bit of a hard sell." As if sensing her mistress's unhappiness, Sophie, the famous belly-dancing dog, jumped on the bed to snuggle with her family. Telly looked at her sad, googly eyes, one facing east, the other west. Her protruding bottom teeth couldn't contain her tiny tongue. She wheezed. Telly patted her matted head. "Not that the two of you weren't wonderful, but..."

"An ex–Playboy Bunny looking for her lost sheep is more entertaining," Gretchen finished forlornly.

"Your performance blew hers out of the water," Telly assured her. Gretchen sniffed loudly, and Telly reached over to grab his glasses so he could see her better. "Gretch, I could get a job teaching."

That was Telly, always trying to make things better whether it was his parents, his brother, or herself—he didn't care what he had to do to make it easier for someone else. Gretchen thought for a minute and decided impulsively to let Telly have a moment too. He loved poker, worshipped the game, the ambiance of the casino, the cool factor, as he called it. What if she encouraged his flight of fancy? Not for long, of course. He wouldn't last—he was such a sweetheart; he couldn't sustain that type of lifestyle. Maybe if he got it out of his system, a regular job might appeal again. What was wrong with helping Telly dream a little? She had an idea, but she had to be careful. The last time he'd gotten caught up in a poker game, he'd become a little obsessed. She would have to make sure she watched him this time and didn't let it get out of hand. Telly was pretty steady, and she did trust that he would make the right decisions in the end. Still, everybody deserved a chance to pursue a dream, even if it wasn't an especially practical one.

"No, Telly." She sat up. "One of us has to have a chance. You always wanted this. Let's try it. Isn't the International Series of Poker coming up in a few weeks?"

"I'll never make the entry fees."

"Use the time to see if you can win enough to enter. Maybe you can do what I couldn't. I know what we need right now." She got up to pad into their kitchenette.

"It feels irresponsible. What if it doesn't work? We don't have much to risk." He considered his options and shook his head. "It goes against everything my parents taught me," Telly called out to her. He heard the freezer open, the jangle of spoons. "What are you doing?"

Gretchen's soft voice carried from the other room. "I agree, Tel. It doesn't feel like real work, but you know, you could do a trial thing, only a month…"

"Or two," he mumbled. "I just have to make it into the Series. I need ten grand." He spoke more to himself than to anyone else. It was his dream. If he could get into a groove, he could support them both comfortably. He hated the place where she worked, but right now, he didn't have options.

"I did say one month, Tel." She was quiet for a few minutes, and then she continued. "We couldn't support a long-term…um…experiment. I mean, I only lasted two weeks."

"Right," Telly yelled and then softened his voice when he realized she was back. He made room for her on the bed. She had a pint of ice cream and two spoons: Gretchen's cure-all.

They dug into the ice cream, taking turns, making sure their spoons didn't clash. Telly was nothing if not polite.

"I don't know. What if I lose too much?" He had never done anything so—what would he call it? Daring? Risky? His parents would have a shit-fit. He could hear them already—it's not steady; the hours are terrible; think of the people you'd be with. *Yeah,* he thought with a snort, *as if the straight and narrow did me any good.* His face darkened.

"Look," Gretchen said, bringing him back. She wanted him to try this; he'd been so unhappy lately. She knew once his confidence was restored, he'd bounce back. He always did. "We'll set a budget and a time limit. We have what…six hundred in the safe?"

"Yeah, but that's for emergencies…"

"Tel. I know what it's for. I'll put in extra hours at the bar, and we'll make it up. Let's treat this like a business. It's not a bad investment for a start-up. We only have to make enough for you to get into the Series." Gretchen smiled. *Then he'll get it out of his system and go for a real job,* she reasoned.

"Aren't you a regular Donald Trump." Telly leaned over to kiss her, enjoying the rum-raisin taste on her lips. "You have to stop me if I get too caught up. You remember what happened the last time?"

"The Poker Game from Hell." Gretchen nodded grimly. Telly got involved in a game in a casino and wouldn't stop, even after he maxed out his credit card to keep buying in. "You lost your head. It was like you were possessed."

"Possessed by the ghost of poker," Telly agreed. "That'll never happen again. So if we plan with what we've got, and say I hit a streak, maybe I'll make it to the Series." It was his lifelong dream to make it into one of the coveted spots of the International Series of Poker, a yearly game that named one winner as the champion of the world. Thousands entered, but there was only a single winner. He closed his eyes and imagined holding the thick gold bracelet and the hefty check for eight million dollars. Boy, that would put them to rights once again. He could feel the bright lights of the cameras, the crowd pressing in on him. He wasn't so redundant…

"Telly…Telly." Gretchen's voice interrupted his fantasy. "It's just a few weeks away. We can do this. If you can't make the entry fee, then Tel, it's over, just like me and belly dancing."

Telly pulled himself up against the headboard. "All right," he said with determination. "I'll do it for both of us. If I qualify for the Series and win, I'll finance your show and then we'll both live our dream. You are so good, Gretchen."

Gretchen nuzzled his ear, tickling him. "Do you remember when your parents thought I was a gold digger?"

"Yeah, well you showed them; you've stuck with me through thick and thin." He pointed to his lip and then his heart. It was a thing between them—sometimes when words didn't work, all they said was thick and thin while pointing to their lips and heart. It was all they needed. He settled in bed, pulling her downward. "I just wish your mom didn't think I was such a jerk."

Gretchen snuggled close. "I love you, Telly. No matter what my mom says, I love you."

Telly wrapped an arm around her, and Sophie the Lhasa settled on his other side. He didn't have a job or reasonable prospects, but he had a great girl and life was good.

***

Time flew by, and before he knew it, the money and the trial period were almost gone. Things did not go as well as Telly had hoped. He lost and lost, and then he lost some more. Oh, there was an occasional win, but he was so far behind the eight ball at this time, it would take a miracle to catch up. Besides, once they paid their bills, he needed stake money again, so his victories didn't buy them much. Gretchen never complained, but he knew she was working two shifts at the bar, and it was time to move on. How long could he ask her to carry the bulk of the load? He turned the corner to the Tango Motel, their temporary home, wearily climbing the concrete steps to the second level. Each room was a sort of suite, with a kitchenette, a bath, a space for a couch with a television, and a pokey bedroom. It was dank and grimy but cheap enough for the two of them, and it accepted dogs. His neighbor stood outside his apartment smoking lazily in the hot night air.

"Evening, Quick Daddy," Telly said politely.

"My man—how'd you do tonight?" Quick Daddy leaned over the iron railings of the balcony, his cigarette dangling from his slender fingers.

Telly shrugged.

"Man, Tel, something's got to give." He pulled off his do-rag, revealing rows of braided hair.

Telly smiled, "Cheryl do that?"

"She like to pretend she still a hairdresser," Quick Daddy replied. "Here come my babydoll now."

Cheryl bounded up the steps two at a time. She was dressed for business in satin hot pants and a sports bra with two shells covering her breasts. She slid a roll of money into Quick Daddy's hand.

Telly nodded. "Hi, Cheryl."

"Hi, Telly. How were the tables tonight?"

Telly responded that the gods of gambling hadn't shined down on him. He never asked Cheryl how her job was. He didn't want to know. It wasn't that he judged her; it was just that he was uncomfortable talking about it.

Cheryl pulled off the waist-length red wig, revealing a cap of short, flattened yellow curls.

"Hard night, babydoll?" Quick Daddy asked sympathetically.

"It's a grind," she replied forlornly, and then she cracked up, causing her boyfriend to laugh with her.

Telly looked at her oddly. "They are hiring down at the mall, Cheryl."

"Doing what?" Cheryl leaned against the railing. "Telly, I make five times the money I did when I worked in an office. And I make my own hours," Cheryl said, laying her hand on his arm. "Don't look that way. I like my work. I don't mind."

Telly was aghast. "You like calling yourself 'The Little Spermaid'?"

"Oh, that's just a gimmick. But it's *my* gimmick. *My* choice. Got it, Telly? Don't you feel sorry for me. I won't stand for it. This is the best way we can save up to buy our own CiCi's Pizza franchise."

"CiCi's Pizza?"

"Everybody's got a dream, Telly. We need fourteen thousand dollars more. By this time next year, you'll be eating pizza on us."

Dreams, it seems, are universal. Everybody has one, Telly thought. "If I make it into the Series and win, then you guys won't have to wait until next year."

"Then you and Gretch will be eating free pizza for the rest of your lives!" Cheryl announced proudly. "Right, Daddy?"

"Whatever you say, babydoll," he agreed, and then he pulled her toward their rooms, leaving Telly to consider the black velvet sky.

CHAPTER FIVE

Telly opened the door of the shabby apartment. His folks wouldn't even visit him here; they were that upset with the place. Still, it was affordable, and he knew they wouldn't be there for long.

Gretchen looked up from the rusty-orange sofa, a romance book in her hands. "How'd you do, Tel?" she asked hopefully.

"Well, I almost won a hand." He threw the key card onto the scarred dresser top where it skidded through the dust. He took off his glasses to rub his tired eyes.

Gretchen stood to embrace him, but he waved her off, pointing to his speckled pants. "Don't come near me till I change." He shrugged. "A bride got sick on me."

Gretchen sighed. "Maybe it's good luck."

"It's *my* luck," Telly responded from the bedroom, changing into sweats. Gretchen heard water running.

"There is always tomorrow…unless you want to think about the job at George's Cab Service." She said it softly, but Telly heard her.

"The Series is next week," he said, as if that explained everything. "I know it's been hard, Gretchen. It's not like

I don't appreciate how you've supported my dream, but I feel so close."

He came out of the bathroom to see Gretchen's lips pursed with disapproval. He felt bad—they had agreed that if he didn't succeed, he would shelve the whole idea. But he just wasn't ready to do that yet.

The cab job…twelve hours a day, six days a week. A steady income, but no shot for real money. Once he took that, his chances for the Series were impossible. They had to last another week, just another week.

"We're so close—registration is Monday." Telly came in to sit on the edge of the couch.

Gretchen closed her book and turned to face him. She had been quiet the last few days. Anybody who knew Gretchen could tell she was concerned. Gretchen had turned inward. She didn't want to burden him with her suspicions, at least not yet, but Telly had to get a real job, really fast. She worried her bottom teeth with her top lip, her hands twisting. This was all her fault in so many ways. It had seemed like a good idea a few weeks ago, but instead of bolstering his confidence, losing so many games was causing Telly to sink to a new low. People made him feel incompetent. It had the opposite effect Gretchen had expected. She had to get him out of that climate before he had a breakdown. She knew Telly, worried about him. It's hard to keep getting up when you are constantly thrown back down. He needed something safe. *How hard can it be to drive a cab?* she thought. A few weeks and he'll be back to his old self. If she were a gambling woman, she would bet money on it. Aside from that, they didn't have time anymore for experiments. Their lives were about to change in a big way. She filed that problem in the back of her head under bad timing, figuring she'd spring it on him when they were more secure. Instead she said, "I know, honey. But we don't have the entry fee anymore. I used it up for the car."

Telly sighed, his cheeks taut, and ran his hands through his hair. "The car…right." Gretchen touched his face. Sophie jumped up to lay her paw against his knee, her bulbous eyes appealing. "So much is resting on me winning, Gretchen. You, Sophie, Cheryl…"

"Cheryl?"

"She wants to open a pizza place. It's a long story, but I don't know, I have a feeling, a good feeling. Something big is going to happen. I can't give up now." Telly took her hands within his own. "Just another few days, and then…I'll give up."

Gretchen stood, her face closed, and pulled her purse from the closet. He was merely putting off the inevitable. It was actually harder watching him lose. Gretchen couldn't understand what he saw in the whole thing. How could he not see what she needed to tell him? She opened her mouth to tell him, but instead huffed angrily, "That's it, Telly!"

Telly looked up, surprised. Gretchen never raised her voice.

"Stop setting impossible standards for yourself. You are always trying to please somebody. You have to stop!"

"I like pleasing you." He smiled, and it broke her mood. She smiled at him warmly. You couldn't stay mad at Telly. He was one of the good guys.

"I like when you please me too." She hugged him. "Take a step back and stop being so hard on yourself. You can't save the world."

"I can barely save myself," Telly said softly.

Gretchen cupped his face. "I think you are the best man I know. When will you realize that? Stop trying so hard. I have to go." She took off his glasses and kissed him gently on the mouth. "Try to get some rest." She rubbed the red spots on each side of his nose and then replaced the glasses gently. "Thick and thin." She kissed each cheek and then turned to leave.

"Where are you going? It's after ten."

"One of the girls called off. I figured we could use the extra money."

"Come on, I'll drive you."

"I didn't pick up the car. We still owe another two hundred. They won't release it."

"OK, that's it. I'll go fill out an application tomorrow. I give up."

Gretchen smiled sadly. "Believe me, Telly. I know how this feels. Look, maybe I can get a payday loan." She added, "For the car, I mean."

"Forget it, Gretch. I knew tonight was my last night. It's over. I'll walk you to the bar."

Gretchen shook her head. "No, you go to sleep. We don't want you looking tired when you go look for a job tomorrow."

Telly shook his head and stood, ready to escort Gretchen the three blocks to the bar where she worked. They held hands the whole way, admiring the midnight sky flecked with silver stars. Telly pointed out constellations. "That's the summer triangle."

Gretchen stopped to peer into the inky darkness. "I don't see it."

"How could you miss it? Look, there's Altair, Vega, and Deneb." He drew an imaginary triangle in the air to show her their location. Gretchen turned to face him.

"You are so smart."

"Yeah, a real Einstein. I'm just a font of useless information."

Gretchen grabbed his face, kissing him and smashing his glasses against his eyelids. "Never say that, Telly. You are the smartest guy I know. I'm patient, and I'm willing to wait for the rest of the world to realize it!"

Telly took her hand. "Come home with me, Gretchen," he said urgently. He had a bad feeling. He didn't want her going into the bar. "Don't go in there."

"Stop. There's a fight this week in town. There'll be a lot of customers tonight. What's wrong?"

"I don't know." Telly looked at the ground, feeling silly. They stood together at the back door near the nasty-smelling garbage. "What time do you get off?"

A red mustang pulled in, spraying gravel everywhere. It jerked to a stop, and Gretchen's boss got out. Rob Couts had a bullet-shaped shaved head, with beefy arms that reminded Telly of Popeye. In fact, that was what Telly called him, at least at home. He was short, but he walked with his hands fisted in a determined stride. He stepped from his car, his beady eyes moving down Gretchen's body, and briefly glanced in Telly's direction. "What's up, Radio?"

"It's Telly," he replied, feeling the hairs go up on his neck.

"I know. I feel funny saying it. Hi, Gretch, you ready for tonight?" He turned to Gretchen, his voice a gravelly caress.

Gretchen's shoulders hunched. "I'm not on for another fifteen minutes," she replied. Telly watched her shrink before his eyes. He reached out to take her fingers loosely within his own. The air felt weighted; an electric current of tension sizzled in the hot air. A cat meowed, breaking the silence.

"You the poker player?"

"I like to play, yes," Telly said defensively.

"Yeah, I bet you're a regular Phil Hellmuth." Rob looked him up and down and then dismissed him. "So I'll see you at the Series, right?"

"The Series?" Telly asked.

"Yeah, doofus. The Series. If you play, you gotta play in that."

"Of course—but I…I think we may have another commitment, right, Gretch?"

Gretchen nodded mutely, her eyes wide. She did not like Rob Couts. Rob stayed longer than he should have, even though he saw Gretchen slide her hand inside Telly's. He looked at their clasped hands and said quietly, "I think it's time for you to leave, Radio."

Gretchen squeezed his hand and said loudly, "Not yet," staring the other man down.

The couple appeared to be having a private moment, but Rob stood watching them. He hawked once, spitting a glob of mucus toward the trash. "If you change your commitments, I'll see you at the Series. Thirteen minutes left," he said abruptly, pushing through them to go inside. He had wide shoulders and wore short-sleeved shirts so you could see the veining on his muscled arms. Telly felt like a gawky kid next to him. Telly straightened his shoulders, but Rob had already dismissed him. He looked at her, trying to catch her eyes in the moonlight. "I'm going for the cab job first thing tomorrow. Are you uncomfortable here? Don't go in."

"It's silly. You know I like my job. He's just got a crush on me this week. He'll move on to Jana next week."

"I don't like the way he was looking at you."

For the first time, his mild-mannered girlfriend bristled. "You think I can't take care of myself? I've been on my own since I was seventeen, Telly. I can take care of myself."

"I never doubted that, Gretch," Telly said honestly. He loved her independence. Gretchen had reunited with her mother just recently, after a lifetime of foster care. Her mother had spent Gretchen's youth in a haze of alcohol abuse and drug addiction.

"Go home, Tel. I'll be back by five." She turned toward the door.

Telly reached into his pocket, opening his wallet to pull out a thinly folded ten-dollar bill. It was his emergency cash. When he'd first gotten his license, his mother had given it to him and insisted that he keep it behind his ID card so he would never be without money. He had never used it and was a little sentimental about it. It made Gretchen's insides melt. Telly would give the shirt off his back if she didn't protect him.

"No, Telly!"

"Don't argue with me." He placed it in her palm. "Call a cab. I mean it, Gretchen. Don't walk home." He placed his finger on her lip and then his heart.

Gretchen whispered, "Thick and thin." She kissed him good-night, waving as he left to walk the few blocks home alone.

CHAPTER SIX

Telly sighed, leaving her. He hated that place. She'd worked there before they met. After they got together, he had gotten her a position serving drinks in the high-roller section of the casino. She was a victim of the take-over, having lost her job as well. She told him he should be grateful Rob took her back. The tips were decent; she got to take home wings for them nightly; and it didn't involve stripping. It wasn't a bad gig, Gretchen insisted. "Believe me," she told him. "I've had worse." He loved her tough resilience. Gretchen was like prairie grass: strong and willing to adapt. His parents had balked in the beginning. She wasn't what they expected for him—no career, no education, no family to speak of. He could do better, they complained. Pliable, moldable Telly stood resistant to his parents for the first time in his life. Their criticism fell on deaf ears, and when he finally told them in his quiet, reasonable way all the reasons he loved Gretchen, they gave in, only to fall under her delightful spell. Gretchen was magic as far as Telly was concerned, and he felt alive when he was with her.

A dog barked, the sound echoing on the deserted street. Telly felt a coldness dance down his spine. He paused to look around. Once, when he was young, he'd felt a weird kind of chill shake his body, and his father had told him someone was "walking on his grave." *Well,* Telly thought as he made a slow 360-degree spin, *someone's break-dancing on it right now.* He stopped, listening for something, and then concentrated on the shuffle of his footsteps. Left, right, left, right, left, left, right, right—he spun…someone was following him. The bleak street stared back at him, devoid of anything. Even the barking dog disappeared. It was silent. The air thickened. Telly strained his ears for any sound but heard nothing. He scanned the street and then picked up his pace with a skip. The additional steps picked up theirs as well. Soon Telly sprinted, the slap of his feet echoed by someone behind him. He faltered, falling to his knee and ripping his pants as he skinned it on the dirty pavement, his breaths coming in huge gulps. Digging his fingers into the blacktop, he rose, craning his neck frantically to look for the person following him. Sweat dripped down his face as he ran, his uneven footsteps echoed by the phantom pursuer. His escape was cut short when he felt a tug on his shirt. Spinning breathlessly, Telly raised his hand to whack someone but turned to the nothingness of the dank Vegas night. The stars mocked him, twinkling down, while he breathed hard, feeling scared and trapped. Telly gulped air, sweat running down his face. It was hot, even at night after the sun went down. The air was sultry, the streetlamps enveloped in a haze. The blare of sirens rent the evening. Shots were fired. The sounds of a Vegas evening back again. He listened to the tinny sound of music coming from a house down the block. The dog commenced its complaint, barking wildly, its pit-bull body hitting a chain-link fence with a resounding crash. Telly shuddered and took a deep, reassuring breath. There was no one there. Stuffing his hands into his pockets, he looked around once more. A man wearing only his boxers and a pair of slippers moved his trash can into the street. They stared hard at each other. Telly raised his hand in a friendly salute. The other man ignored him and turned to head back into the buttery light of his front door. Telly watched him closely, the door shutting out the inviting light. He headed for home.

* * *

Telly walked into the apartment, the television bathing the room in an eerie blue glow. He looked, his eyes widening as he stared at the screen. *Why is the television on?* he thought nervously. Grabbing the remote, he pressed the power button but the TV remained on. Telly squeezed the power button so hard, it got jammed in the plastic of the remote. Frustrated, he chucked it onto the orange sofa. They must have left the television on when they'd departed. Telly thought that was strange. They had never done that before. Gretchen was very careful with waste. He changed from pants to a pair of shorts and washed his knee, wincing when he cleaned the abrasion, and then he covered the scrape with a bandage. He kicked off his shoes, grabbed a beer, and flopped on the worn couch, stuffing a flattened pillow beneath his head. The Poker Channel was on, and Telly snorted, thinking Gretchen would never have left that on knowing how cruel it would be. She must have thought it was just another sports channel. The sportscaster droned on about different contestants. Telly recognized the old guy he'd played with tonight at the Bellagio, the one who said if he played at the Series he wanted to sit next to him. The old guy was being interviewed, and Telly's eyelids drooped. He watched Friday end and the weekend start. The Series was officially three days away, and he would be driving some other guy to play in it.

"The annual International Series of Poker's Main Event kicks off this Monday. The biggest and brightest stars in the poker world will be in attendance. One who won't be returning is the legendary Clutch Henderson, who passed away of a massive coronary at last year's final table."

"A sad day in Vegas," said the other newscaster, Kevin-something. Telly listened absently, turning away from the screen. He had a vague memory of the Henderson guy dying right before he lost. "A tragic day. Do you recall his hand, Stu?"

"Indeed I do: four kings were at that table that night," he intoned sadly.

"FOUR KINGS, you asshole?"

Telly's eyes popped open at the expletive. It was loud. It didn't get bleeped. Telly rolled up. The voice sounded as if it were in the room. He looked wildly around. Laughter filled the apartment.

"He must be senile, that fat bastard. I had three kings," Clutch chuckled. "Sheesh, Stuie, what happened to you?"

Telly turned to see a vague outline of a man on the sofa next to him. He was old, with a shock of white hair and a lean, wolfish look. He crushed Telly's beer can, burped loudly, and said, "Go get us another one, son. I'm powerfully thirsty."

Telly looked over his shoulder to see Sophie sleeping on her little round dog bed. He called her name softly. For Chrissakes, she barked at everything. Sophie looked up, her eyes refracting the light. "Do you see anything strange, girl?"

Sophie snuffled noisily, placed her head back into the well of her body, and began to snore again.

"The dog don't care about me."

There was no mistake—he heard a voice, clear as day. Telly blanched; his skin tightened on his scalp as if it were being pulled back from his face. He scrambled up the arm of the couch, while the image wavered as it shook with good-natured laughter. *I'm losing my mind,* Telly thought feverishly.

The television droned on. "Clutch had two kings with one on the table," Kevin corrected his colleague.

"Oh, listen, listen," Clutch stood, moving closer to the TV to make the sound louder. "This guy was paying attention to me that night. Like my grandpappy Buster used to say, 'You can judge a man by the amount of hair in his ears.'"

"That makes no sense," Telly told him.

"The way I see it," Stu shook his head, "Clutch may have had three kings, but he was the king of the table that night. He is the king of poker."

"The king of poker?" The apparition stood before Telly. "I'm the fucking emperor of poker! The caesar of poker! The khan of pok—say, what's wrong with you, boy?" He bent low to see Telly's frozen face. Clutch reached out, causing Telly to lean back and slide off the couch, landing with a thud. The older man crouched down, but Telly skittered away, his hand scrambling for his cell phone. He pulled it down but couldn't get the screen to wake up.

"It's no use; it's dead. Like me," the spirit told him.

Telly crawled toward the bedroom. In a burst, he scrambled on all fours, his forgotten skinned knee raw with pain. His glasses were off, so everything had a muted, fuzzy look. He could barely see. He hurried into the next room, slamming the door behind him. His back against the door, he pressed every button on the phone, his breath harsh. His asthma came back, tightening his airways, and soon he was wheezing like a set of old bellows. His pulse pounded in his head, his hands shaking. He was tired.

He figured he must have been sleeping. *I never should've eaten yesterday's wings—who knows how old they were?* he thought frantically.

Placing a hand on the floor, he made to rise, only to find himself face-to-face with the green, glowing person. "You better take your spray, man. You're noisier than a freight train."

This time, Telly closed his eyes and screamed as loud as his closed throat would allow. It came out like a reedy clarinet, and Clutch covered Telly's mouth to silence him.

The last thing Telly remembered was that the cold hands didn't feel bad at all.

Telly came to awareness on his lumpy bed, a wet cloth on his head making runnels of water that were soaking the pillow. He felt clammy. When he sat up, the rag fell into a sodden heap in his lap. The man was sitting on the edge of the bed reading a newspaper.

"Beetlejuice, Beetlejuice, Beetlejuice..." Telly repeated frantically.

"Aw, kid, that don't work. That's fake. All that crap is fake from the movies. It's nothing like that," Clutch held out a ghostly hand. "Don't go all white and faint again, now. Listen...Telly—"

"You know my name?"

"I've been watching you for a while." He picked up Telly's hand to shake it. "Clutch Henderson. Nice to meet you."

Telly pulled his hand away, chilled with the contact. He looked around the room, squinting at the digital clock to see the time.

"It's two, and no, you're not dreaming. Here, put on your glasses so you can see me better."

"I don't want to see you better." Telly put on his glasses anyway, blinking owlishly.

Clutch ignored him with good-natured bonhomie. He reached over to pick up a book on the nightstand. "I like your reading material." The ghost held up his last book; a photograph of Clutch himself on the back cover mocked him.

Telly opened and closed his mouth like a hooked trout. Clutch pointed to the author's picture. "Yep, it's me all right."

Telly reached out a hand to touch Clutch's knee. His hand went right through him, but his fingers stiffened with cold. He pulled back, rubbing them to warm them back to life.

"What's happening? Am I having a breakdown?"

"Nope. Something happened tonight—something special. I was walking along and saw you make a wish." Clutch held up his hands, wiggling his fingers. He reached forward, pulling a coin from Telly's ear. "Your wish became our wish."

"But you're dead. You can't have wishes."

"Who says?" Clutch demanded. "Maybe I died with my wish. They don't disintegrate, just because we die. Wishes have lives of their own. You should know that."

He did know that. Telly's wish was a living, breathing thing that he carried with him all hours of the day. "What has that got to do with me?"

"You and I have the same wish, and we're going to make it come true together."

"That's crazy. You're dead. You're not alive. You can't play poker."

"Well, you're alive, and you can't play for shit either. Together, we're going to win this game."

"You're nuts!" Telly screamed, the veins popping on his neck. He jumped up to pace the room. "No, I'm nuts! I'm certifiable. Gretchen's going to have to commit me."

"Well, if that's true, at least you won't have to drive a cab."

"How did you know that?" Telly demanded.

"I know everything." Clutch came nose to nose with him, his blue eyes glaring. "That's how we are going to win—I can see and hear everything." He winked. "I can see the other players' cards. I'm gonna tell you what to do. My grandpappy always said, 'A man's got to have eyes in his ears and ears in his eyes.'"

"That's just about the dumbest…hey, that's cheating!"

"So what? All you need is a chip and a chair, and I'm going to take you all the way to the top."

"Are you asking me to sell my soul? Are you the devil?" He sat down on the edge of the bed.

"Now I know you're nuts. That shit only happens on the television, Telly." The ghost moved closer to him on the bed. Telly skittered away. Clutch asked gently, "Don't you want to know what it feels like to win?"

"You are the devil," Telly said softly.

"Just imagine what Gretchen's going to say when you give her that big, fat, yellow diamond."

Telly gasped. "How did you know…"

"I told you—I know everything."

"It's cheating. I don't cheat." Telly stood to pace the room.

"Neither does Gretchen…yet?" Clutch said cryptically. He waved his hands, and the television in the bedroom went on. It was the bar, and Gretchen was setting up a tray of drinks. "Sit back and watch the show, Telly."

Telly stared wide-eyed as the seedy bar filled the television screen like a cheap sitcom. He grabbed the remote, clicking it to the off position, fear lodging in his chest when the picture remained. His jaw dropped when he heard Gretchen speak.

"Glad those losers left," she said as she placed cash on the bar.

Chrissy, Gretchen's friend, leaned against the bar separating a group of bar tabs. Assorted piles of change were spread across the counter. She looked at the C-note Gretchen had placed on the bar. "What you'd do to earn that?"

"Dazzled them with my charming wit." Gretchen laughed. "I gave them coupons to the nearest strip club. They were so grateful, it was pathetic."

"You don't have to split that with me," Chrissy told her. She was a whey-faced waitress with a fake diamond stud in her nose and a matching one on her upper lip.

"We decided to pool everything, Chris. We can't change the rules now."

"No one ever got nothing that big here. You ran your ass off for them tonight."

Gretchen shrugged. "That's the job."

"You might as well keep it—you're going to need it. If Telly's luck doesn't change, you're going to have to ask for more hours. I don't know why you put up with his crap."

Gretchen shook her head. "Telly's a great guy. I'll never leave him," she said with a smile.

"He's a loser, just like every other loser in this city. Listen, Gretchen, I'll ditch Jack. He's deadweight too."

Telly winced at the description. He wondered if Gretchen thought of him as deadweight.

"He's working as a teller! In a bank! Sheesh, what an asshole," Chrissy finished. "Minimum wage."

"He's trying to use his education to get him a career; you have to give him credit."

"He'd be better off being an electrician, but noooo. He had to waste all that money on that online college."

"Well, I admire Jack for trying," Gretchen told her.

"By spending thirty thousand dollars to work for a shitty wage? No thank you. It'll take forever to pay back those school loans. Listen." Chrissy leaned closer. "Let's get a place together. We can pool everything and move into a better neighborhood. We don't need these creeps."

"You don't mean that, Chrissy. Jack's sweet, like Telly. Besides, I love Telly and…and…" She paused as if she had something to share and then shook her head. "Anyway, tomorrow he's going to George and taking the cab driver job."

Chrissy pulled her lips downward in a grimace, then shook her head. She glanced around the room, her eyes falling on the boss. "You don't have to put up with cab driver's pay, anyway. Rob can't keep his eyes off you."

Telly observed Gretchen looking at the manager. He was sitting at a table in the rear, his laser eyes watching her intently. He raised a glass slowly, nodding for her to come closer. "Ugh, I have to ask for more hours, and I hate when he does this," Gretchen complained.

"He wants to take you out, and he won't stop until you give him what he wants."

"There are laws that say he can't do that!" Gretchen hissed.

Telly smiled as he watched. "Good girl, Gretch."

Chrissy laughed bitterly. "Yeah, sure, honey. I got a good bridge to sell you too. That's why we women outnumber them two to one in management," she finished sarcastically. "Look, either Telly has to make enough to get you out of this shitbox, or you better get ready to make that bonehead happy. I read the book, and it don't look like a happy ending for you."

"Gretchen!" Rob jiggled his glass at her. "Get me a shot."

Telly saw Gretchen sigh, take a deep breath, and walk over with a bottle of tequila. She reached over to take the glass from his hands, but he caught her fingers, turning her hand palm up. Rob walked his fingers over her sensitive skin, and Gretchen impatiently made to grab for his glass. He held it out of her way, his face inches from her breast.

"I got customers waiting; do you want a refill or not?"

Rob handed her the glass, a smirk on his face. A faint shadow of dark hair outlined a horseshoe shape on his head. Telly saw Gretchen observing Rob's wide forehead, wondering if she realized that if he let it grow in, he'd be bald. He smiled when he saw her smirk at her boss's bald head.

"What's so funny?" Rob demanded.

"I'm tired, Rob. It's been a long night. Is it possible for me to get extra hours next week?"

"I'd like an extra night." Rob smiled wolfishly. "How about Tuesday?"

Gretchen shook her head. "No, that would cut into Sylvie's hours. Besides, everybody's consumed with the Series. Tips will be slow."

"I'm not talking about *here,* Gretchen. I'm having a party."

"Oh. I don't usually do the private stuff. Aren't you having Chrissy and her girlfriend work that?"

"I wasn't talking about you *working* for me there. I figured you could come as my guest."

Telly watched Rob's eyes strip her as he downed the shot, slamming the glass on the table.

"Telly—"

"I didn't invite Telly," he told her, reaching out to lay his hand on her hip.

Gretchen sidestepped away, shaking her head.

"You refusing work?" Rob said with a menacing growl.

"You said it wasn't work."

"Did I say that? I don't recall. I said I'm having a party, and I asked you to come," he said with a wide smile that bordered on unfriendly.

Telly turned to Clutch. "I've seen enough; you don't have to leave this on. Gretchen would never cheat." The screen went dark.

***

Gretchen grabbed a wet rag and wiped the stained surface of the bar, angry at Rob and the position he was putting her in. There were no jobs around town. She was on the northern side of thirty, competing with twentysomethings who could juggle bottles like a circus act. Those were the ones who got hired. Gretchen couldn't sing, barely danced, and just yesterday she'd spied a gray hair at her temple. Thank goodness she was blond at least. At this point, she couldn't even afford to go to a beauty parlor to hide it with color. She closed her eyes, willing herself not to cry, and remembered her new complication. Any way she looked at this thing, it didn't look promising. What was she thinking?—she knew how Rob had been eyeing her the last few weeks. If Telly had gotten the taxi job then, she'd be out of here and have the luxury to find something at a reasonable pace, even pick and choose. It wasn't his fault; she hadn't complained. Hadn't wanted to worry him. Telly was such a sweet guy who had fallen in love with her even though she wasn't as educated as he was. He was solid middle class, came from a nice family, and had gone to college. Gretchen had spent a lifetime living in foster care. Never completing tenth grade, she'd fled her last home when her foster father had tried to rape her. She worked hard, never giving in to the temptation for the easy money Vegas offered in the streets. Gretchen had cleaned offices and worked at dead-end retail jobs, finally taking the bartending job in the evenings to supplement her income. It ended up paying her better than all the other jobs put together. Only Rob had bought the little bar, and things started going downhill after that. It didn't take a genius to know what Rob wanted from her. Gretchen bit her lower lip, sound receding so that she felt trapped in a bubble. Telly *had to* get that job tomorrow. He had to, because there was no way she could put up with this. Thick and thin, and it was fast becoming so thin you could see through it. She sighed.

"I'll see you Tuesday. Wear something nice," Rob said to her, retreating back. She heard the echoes of his laughter all the way from the other side of the bar.

CHAPTER SEVEN

"What am I going to do?" Telly walked in a circle, not knowing where to go. "Gretchen..." he sighed.

"Stop doing that; you're making me dizzy," Clutch ordered. "I'm gonna tell you what we're going to do."

"*We're* not doing anything. You're not real."

"I thought we established exactly what I am. I am here to help you."

"I don't know you," Telly said forlornly. He ran his hands through his hair. "I don't know who you are."

"You've read at least one of my books. Believe me, you know me pretty well."

"I read...I read all your books."

"Then there's no issue. We're practically family."

"But you're dead. You can't help me. It's probably the wings. I knew I shouldn't have eaten the wings."

"Wings had nothing to do with this, Telly." Clutch paused and thought of the white-haired angel with the huge feathered wings. "Well, maybe they do, but not the way you think."

"I don't know what to think. This is crazy." Telly sprinted to the bathroom, slammed the door, and leaned up against it, hyperventilating.

"Now listen here, kid. If I could walk through the motel door, I can sure as hell walk through a flimsy bathroom door. Calm down before you ruin everything. Can't have two dead poker players."

"Dead!" Telly exploded. He glanced up to look at his white face in the mirror. A cool breeze ruffled the hair at his neck. Telly knew Clutch was right next to him, but only his face stared back from the mirror.

"You know I'm there. You can feel me, and if you look to your left you'll see me. Look, Telly, I have all the time in the world. I'm not going anywhere until we work this thing out."

Telly turned to face the older man. "What do you want from me?" he whispered frantically.

"That's better. We're going to play poker together."

"Where? How?" Telly shook his head. "Doesn't matter. I retired tonight."

"You lost tonight. Tomorrow you are going to win."

"I'm not good at it. I give up. I'm going for a job in…"—he looked at his wristwatch and sighed—"…seven hours."

"In four hours, I promise you that you are going to be sitting with a pile of chips that will bring you halfway to your seat at the Series."

Telly shook his head. "No way. I'm not that good." He gestured at his pocket. "I'm out of money. No stake."

"Minor issues."

"Maybe to you," Telly said hotly as he left the bathroom. "The fact is, I'm no good at it. I'm a loser!" he shouted.

Someone pounded on the thin walls and yelled, "Quiet, loser!"

"See?" Telly gestured to the wall. "The guy in 4A agrees."

"Pah. That don't mean anything, kid. I can coach you. I can teach you the playbook."

"Right," Telly said. "Well, thank you for coming."

"You're going to throw it all away," Clutch said with disgust. "You have the greatest player in the history of the game begging to teach you, and you want to toss me out like yesterday's trash."

"May I remind you, Clutch: you didn't win."

"Broke my heart." Clutch touched his chest, his grim face sincere. "No, really, caused a massive heart attack."

"Why? Why are you doing this? What could you do with the money?"

Clutch walked over to the dusty dresser. His slender fingers drew circles in the grime. Motes lifted to fly around him, and he seemed to glow softly.

"Some things are not about money. I've made millions in my lifetime. I spent part on booze, part on broads." He paused with a smile. "As Buster used to say, 'The rest I spent foolishly.'"

He waited for Telly to laugh. The younger man stared blankly at him.

Clutch sighed. Boy, was this one dumb. "All right, I'll tell ya. I want the bracelet. It's always been about the bracelet."

"Jewelry? This is about jewelry?"

"You looked at that expensive ring for Gretchen today. Ain't nothing more than carbonized rock. It's the symbol of what it represents. For you, the diamond is a token of your success—your love for her, what Gretchen means to you. That bracelet represents my achievement."

"But I'll be the one wearing it if I win," Telly said flatly.

Clutch shrugged and then replied, "*When* you win."

Telly considered the faded apparition before him. His eyes rested on the avocado green carpet that clashed with the raspberry polyester bedspread. Gretchen had bought it at the Home Store in an effort to make the place look more…well, homey. She placed oversized pillows on the hard orange couch. In the corner, a hanging light fixture swayed drunkenly, even though there was no breeze in the room. Telly shivered. He hated this place. He missed his old life—missed having Gretchen cooking in the neat little kitchen with rich, dark espresso-colored cabinets he had purchased to match the quartz countertops that were lit up from below. Everything was controlled by a remote—he had wired the entire house. He could turn on anything from the alarm to his colored mood lights in his pool. It was sexy in a nerdy kind of way. Now the only thing he controlled was a twenty-inch television that turned off every time the manager forgot to pay the cable bill.

"Come on, Telly," Clutch urged. "You're gonna lose Gretchen. I showed you. You really will," he wheedled.

"That would never happen. Gretchen's true blue; she's fearless," Telly said earnestly. "Besides, I don't have a dime to buy into a game. That is, even if I believed all of this was really happening."

Clutch laughed, coming closer, so that Telly could feel the cold shivers of his breath dancing down his cheek.

"It's two in the morning."

"We got hours ahead of us."

"I don't have any money. I'm broke."

"Ask your friend."

"Friend? What friend?" Telly found himself propelled outside his unit to the one next door. "Wait, I don't have a jacket."

"Pussy." Clutch pushed him along the narrow walkway and pointed to his neighbor's door.

"I get cold in the casinos…Quick Daddy!" Telly squeaked as he knocked on the door. He whispered to Clutch, "You want me to ask…"

The door suddenly opened. "Telly, what up, man? You pissed off the dude in 4A with all your noise." Quick Daddy stood in the doorway, his brown eyes heavy with sleep. "You gonna be wakin' the dead with all that banging around. What you need, lil' brother?"

"Ask him! Go ahead, ask." Clutch poked his shoulder.

"Stop that," Telly said impatiently.

Quick Daddy pushed his scrawny upper body through the opening. "You got someone there?"

"No. Ow!" Telly felt the long hairs at the back of his head being pulled.

"Who's there?" Cheryl's disembodied voice drifted out.

Telly's pinky twisted backward into a death-defying arc of gravity not unlike a Cirque du Soleil dancer.

Daddy watched and then commented, "Better eat some bananas, man. You need potassium."

"What?" Telly struggled with his defiant hand.

"For cramps. You need something, Tel?"

"Just do it!" Clutch shouted.

Telly winced, his lips pressed in a thin line.

"Say it. 'I need five hundred dollars.' Say it!"

"I don't want…"

"Don't want what, Telly? It's late."

Daddy was interrupted by Cheryl's shrill voice. "It's freakin' hot—you're letting out all the air conditioning. Close the freakin' door!"

"Aw, baby, I hate when you talk like that." Daddy turned to face inward.

"Just say it." Clutch grabbed Telly's earlobe, tweaking it.

"I need five hundred dollars!" Telly exploded. Everything stopped at once; the landing was so quiet that only the distant police sirens could be heard.

"What, Telly? You need money?"

"No, no…I'm sorry." Telly backed away from the door to bump into a cold, solid wall that prevented further retreat.

Daddy pulled a wad of folded bills from his pocket. "Why didn't you say earlier? Forget it, man." He brushed off Telly's embarrassment. "You know I always offered it to you."

"You see what I mean?" a voice sneered into his ear.

"That was unnecessary," Telly whispered back.

"No, no it's necessary." Daddy smiled. "You found that doctor for me when I busted my toe. I'll never forget that, Telly." He peeled off five hundred-dollar bills, looked at Telly, and continued talking. "I'm so glad you finally let me help you. What's it for?"

Telly gaped at Daddy, words failing him.

"You know what? I don't want to know. Here you go, man." He placed the money in Telly's slack hand. "You don't have to pay me back. You got that, Tel? I'm happy to help. Nothing, not even interest. Happy to help you, man."

"Wow! Lucky money." Clutch slapped his back, sending shivers up and down his spine. "Come on, son. We got a game to play. As Buster used to say, 'We got fish to fry and grease in your pocket!'"

"I'm beginning to really dislike this Buster," Telly grumbled.

CHAPTER EIGHT

Telly stood on a landing that led to the Mirage poker room. The tropical-themed carpeting swirled beneath his feet in a collage of green and peach. A short waitress came over to ask if he wanted a drink. At Clutch's appreciative, guttural growl, Telly turned to tell him to be quiet. The girl observed his gesture to thin air and then skittered away from him, her black miniskirt fluttering above her thin legs.

Clutch poked him from behind. "Never mind the drinks. Go down and register."

"Forget it. I don't want to do this. I'm going home." Telly spun to face the exit, but he couldn't move. His feet were stuck fast to the floor."Let go of me," he whispered urgently. It was hot. It was summer. He didn't know why he had taken his jacket, but he felt like it gave him an extra layer of protection. Without it, he felt exposed. He whipped off his jacket, but it got caught on his arm. Telly tried to peel it off, but it was adhered to him like a second skin. "Are you doing that?" he demanded. "Well, I don't care, because…"

"Do you have a problem?" A man in a suit with the multicolored palm-tree logo on the lapel watched him intently. "Can I help you with something?" Steven Marks—or so his badge said—inquired.

"Tell him you're hungry. Maybe we'll get some steaks," Clutch whispered with excitement.

"I'm not hungry!" Telly shouted.

"Great. Do you have a player's card?" the casino employee asked.

Automatically Telly reached into his pocket to hand over his card.

"Telly Martin. I've seen you here before. Do you have a host?"

"Host?"

"Yes, a host. Someone to take care of you. You know what I'm going to do for you, Telly?" Steven Mark asked.

Telly shook his head, dumbfounded.

"Are you on vacation, or do you live here?" Steven asked. "Not that it matters—tonight we are running a special promotion for the poker room. I am going to comp your entrance to the Wednesday night tourney. It's a hundred-dollar value, " he added.

"You see." Clutch prodded him from behind. "They're practically throwing money at you."

"Why?" Telly asked. He had played there for over a month and had never been noticed.

"Everybody needs somebody to take care of them sometimes. Here's my card. If you need anything, give me a call," the host told him with a smile.

He handed Telly a brightly printed glossy paper and pointed to the registration desk.

Then Telly heard both Steven and Clutch say, in unison, "What are you waiting for? Go play."

Clutch's voice was very close to his ear, blabbering away, as Telly signed in. "Now listen, we're going to go cash in, and you do everything I tell you."

Telly ignored him. He felt a hand press down on his shoulder. "You got that?"

Telly wouldn't look in his direction. He whispered, "Yes."

"I said, you got that?" Clutch roared.

Telly hissed back, "I said yes!"

The table in front of him paused. A few men looked up, and then they went back to their game.

All around him was a sea of tables filled with people playing. The room was not loud, but there was the babble of multiple games going on. There was no small talk; the occasional "I raise" or "Call" broke the constant hum. Smoke hung heavy on the air from the adjoining casino, and Telly's eyes stung until they adjusted. He felt tired, his feet leaden.

"I really don't want to do this," he muttered forlornly.

"Ask if there are any seats open at the no-limit table," Clutch told him.

"No limit—are you nuts? I can't do no limit. Besides, five hundred dollars won't last two hands there."

"It'll take us forever to make the ten grand you need otherwise," Clutch hissed into his ear. "Just do what I tell you!"

Telly rolled his eyes. "I won't even last fifteen minutes at a twenty-five-dollar table. The money will evaporate."

"I'm going to evaporate and leave you here with your finger up your ass if you don't listen to me," Clutch argued back.

Robert Maxwell smoothed his shirt over his potbelly. *Another crazy talking to himself in the middle of the floor.* He approached Telly with a wide smile. Clamping his arm around Telly, he pulled the reluctant man toward the no-limit table.

"Did I hear you say *no limit*? Right this way, sir."

"I've never played this high before, and I'm only playing for a short time. I don't know…"

"You don't know what?" Robert asked him. "You really have to find a seat. You are distracting the other players. Would you rather sit on the balcony and watch?"

Clutch materialized in a vaporous form for the first time since they had entered the casino. He had a drink in one hand and was gazing distractedly at the crowd. Crooning a Sinatra tune, he looked at Telly and winked. "Don't be afraid," he whispered.

Telly looked wildly around to see if anyone else saw the spirit. People were engaged in their play, seemingly unaware of Clutch standing in their midst.

"Do you see an old white-haired guy?" Telly asked the host.

"I see a lot of old white-haired guys. Are you looking for someone in particular?" Maxwell responded.

Telly opened his mouth, and Clutch shook his head and waved a finger at him. "You're flirting with being locked up—watch."

Clutch unzipped his pants, bent over, and did a complete full moon in the middle of the casino. His slacks around his ankles, he did a shuffling polka around the tables in front of Telly. The games continued; his antics interrupted nothing. "I told you, Telly, nobody can see me but you."

"I think I've seen enough," Telly said out loud.

"Don't you want to play?" the host asked. "You just got here. Why don't you take a seat?" Robert insisted, worried about the demented look in the younger man's eyes. "Are you OK, sir?"

Clutch pointed to an empty chair. "Sit. Down."

The room narrowed to the green chair, and all noise became muted. "This is crazy," Telly muttered.

Clutch held up his skeletal fingers, wiggling his pointer. "If you don't try, you'll never know."

Robert gestured to the empty chair. "Someone is going to fill this seat. We can't hold it for you."

Telly slid into the chair, tentatively putting his forearms on the edge of the table.

"Evening." He nodded to the players. He turned to the player next to him, an older woman with three chins and frizzled gray hair. "You from Vegas?"

"Don't talk to them!" Clutch shouted. "Listen to me."

Telly placed his bankroll on the table; his hands were clammy, and he had broken out into a sweat.

Meaty paws grabbed the cash, counted it out, and replaced it with three stacks of twenty-five-dollar green chips. Telly pulled the chips close to him with shaky fingers.

The cards flew across the table, and Telly reached out to look at them.

"Pick 'em up by curling them upward. Not so high, stupid!" Clutch looked at Telly's cards. "Not bad," he said, eyeing the two nines. "You're in a good position."

"I know," Telly agreed.

"You know what?" a scruffy, heavyset man wearing a jet-colored toupee demanded. Telly stared at the matted mess on his head. The man's natural gray hair curled under the very black and flattened wig he wore. He was older, with a huge nose dominating the fleshy folds of his face. He wore a heavy, flat, linked gold chain with an ornate medallion that Telly couldn't make out.

"What?" Telly asked.

"What do you know?" he spat out belligerently.

Telly shrugged. "I don't know."

"You said, 'I know.'" He placed his cards down to stare at Telly's face, his small eyes narrowing.

"I know when to hold 'em," Telly sang sheepishly.

"Raise!" Clutch yelled. "You're holding up the game. Say, 'I raise.' Say it now."

"I raise," Telly blurted.

"Very well. How much?" the dealer questioned.

"I raise one dollar."

Two players cursed loudly. The old lady clicked her tongue at Telly. "There is a minimum bet, young man," she told him.

"The minimum bet is fifty dollars," the dealer said impatiently.

Telly's mind was blank—a big, dark abyss filled with nothing. "I can't…fifty dollars…I…"

"Telly, fold this hand and meet me in the bathroom. Now."

"I don't have to go to the bathroom," Telly said to the table.

"Who you talking to, boy?" The heavy man with the toupee half rose from his seat.

"Do you raise?" the dealer interrupted. "Anyone have a problem letting this guy fold until he figures out where he wants to be?"

Telly looked at the hostile faces observing him, the dealer's impassive expression, and Clutch standing impatiently by the restroom door. Toupee man shrugged and said, "Go ahead, fold already."

"You coming?" Clutch waved him over.

Telly gently placed his cards on the green baize. "I fold," he said softly, and then he rose to follow Clutch. "I'll be back in a minute."

"This is bullshit; they let anybody play now," the heavy player complained. "I play at the higher limits to avoid the creeps."

"Creeps have money too," the gray-haired woman added. "Well, I raise; let me see your cards." She smiled.

"Why you made me fold pocket nines, I'll never understand," Telly complained as he followed Clutch into the men's room.

"Go to the last stall," Clutch ordered.

"Can't we just leave?" Telly implored.

Two guys eyed Telly warily. He seemed oblivious to their stares as he unhappily entered the last unoccupied stall.

"Keep your voice down; you're spooking the people in here," Clutch warned him.

Telly laughed. "Me spooking people! You're funny."

"Let's get out of here. He's probably been drinking," he heard someone say.

"Now listen to me, partner. You want to win? I want to win too. We just started our little marathon, and you're screwing around."

"Me? *I'm* screwing around?" Telly shouted.

"Hey. Get a room." He heard the door slam.

"You're stuck with me," Clutch continued, despite the interruption.

"I know. I know I'm stuck with you," Telly said forelornly.

"Dude," a voice called from the next stall.

"You have to listen to what I'm telling you, Telly. You have to pay attention to me."

"Well it's hard," Telly complained.

"Dude!" the voice implored. "I don't want to hear this."

"I know, Telly, but the only way we can do this is if we do it together. As my grandpappy used to say, 'You have to put your trust in the cards.'"

"I'm getting mighty sick and tired of this," Telly ground out.

"Oh man, they let everybody in here," came the agonized reply from the next stall.

"It's hard to trust you when I don't even know if you're real." Telly continued, not aware of the other patrons in the rest room. He was miserable.

"Oh, dude. You poor guy." It was the guy in the next stall again.

"My glasses are steaming up!" Telly said forlornly.

"Just take a deep breath, Telly, and relax," Clutch urged, taking the glasses and cleaning them with his shirttail.

"I am relaxed," Telly responded.

"There you go," the guy in the next stall said.

"This isn't rocket science, Tel. It's not hard at all," Clutch said reasonably.

"I know it's not hard," Telly agreed.

"OK." He heard the door in the next stall slam. "TMI. My turn to exit."

Clutch and Telly were oblivious to the empty bathroom. "Poker," Clutch informed him, "is a lot like sex. Everyone thinks they're the best at it, but most don't have a clue what they're doing…"

"Did Grandpa Buster say that?"

"No, I did," Clutch said confidently.

"In the end, it's still cheating," Telly told him softly. "None of this counts."

"It's a means to an end."

"I don't even know what that means," Telly replied, exasperated.

"Everybody uses something to win. Some people count cards; others watch for your tells," Clutch explained.

"Oh, I know all about tells," Telly said. "You watch for patterns to see how the players react, and then you can get a fair idea of what their cards are. That's not cheating."

"Well, lookie what we got here. A real expert in the game of poker. I got news for ya, partner. Everybody cheats! Half the population is here without their better half knowing what they are doing. They smudge the numbers on their taxes. You want to tell me if a dealer makes a mistake and gives them extra chips, they're going to say something? All I'm doing is hedging your bets. You can walk out of here right now, and it's over…like we never met. Go back to that shithole you came from. Take that crappy job. Continue waiting for your luck to change. But don't you see? There *is no* luck. You have to make your own luck. You need to win. *I* need to win. *Gretchen* needs you to win. I'm telling you, kid. You're going to lose her."

Telly sighed heavily. Gretchen. He couldn't lose Gretchen. She was the best part of his life.

"Now what are you going to do?" Clutch asked.

"Listen to you."

"Right. Don't make conversation with the players. Look at them, Telly. Really look at them. Their goal is to take your money. They are watching you, reading your reactions. Everything you say or do is a clue to what you're holding. Poker isn't gambling."

Telly looked up at him skeptically.

"No, really. Poker is an intense psychological evaluation based on reading your opponent. Poker is not about the cards or even luck as much as it's about making decisions based on experience and instinct."

"Did Buster teach you that?"

"No, Buster just spoke a whole lot of horseshit. I learned that from experience."

"Yeah, but I don't have much of that."

"But I do." Clutch rested his hand on Telly's shoulder. "This is not about the money. This is not about winning. You learn how to play poker, Tel, and you will get anything you want, anywhere. Now let's go out and kick some ass."

* * *

"Look who's back—the chatterbox," the man with the toupee announced.

Telly ignored the remark as he seated himself. He glanced up to see Clutch circling the table like a shark.

"You ready to play now?" triple chin asked him.

"Big blind's on you," the dealer told him, which meant Telly had to be the first to throw in money to play the hand.

"Right." He looked up to see Clutch mouth the word *fifty* with a nod. He slid two green chips into the pot. "Fifty dollars."

"OK, kid," the man next to him said with a smirk. "Let's play poker."

The cards came at him as if in slow motion. He watched the older woman look at him.

He felt Clutch's presence at his elbow as he lifted the cards.

"Jack ten suited. Not bad on the big blind." He heard the words echo in his head. "Telly, don't repeat what I just said."

A smile tugged at Telly's lips, but then he caught the chin lady watching him closely, so he relaxed his face to be expressionless. He heard Clutch tell him he was a good boy, with a hint of approval.

Toupee man next to him glanced at his cards, which were covered by his palm. He heard Clutch mutter, "Move your hands, Elvis, so I can see."

Telly watched intently as he licked his lips and then pulled at the gray hair of his sideburns. The man was oblivious to his observance, so Telly lowered his eyes and stole a look at the elderly woman. She was watching him with interest. She smiled and then drummed her fingers impatiently. She had a huge wart high on her cheek with coarse black hairs growing out of it. Telly stared at it with fascination.

A finger flicked his ear, and he heard Clutch say, "Stop staring at her wart; that won't tell you anything. She's got nothing anyway. Watch, she's going to fold. She drums her fingers and then she'll fold. Her name's Ramona Heart. Most people call her Black Widow."

Telly watched in astonishment as her turn came and she folded. There were a few other players at the table. An Asian guy with dark glasses glanced at his hand, his face blank, as he shuffled the cards beneath his fingers. He said "call" so softly that Telly had to lean forward in order to hear him better.

A young kid wearing a hoodie and an expensive Rolex watch casually flipped a black hundred-dollar chip into the pot. Telly heard Clutch say, "Come to papa...Telly, build the pot, baby."

The pile in the center of the table grew substantially after the flop, which revealed a seven of diamonds, a jack of clubs, and a nine of diamonds.

Clutch whispered urgently, "You have top pair and a belly buster." Telly shrugged, and Clutch explained, "Belly buster means you need an eight for a straight. But we've got jacks; we're good, kid."

Another man, dressed head to toe in powder-blue polyester, rifled his chips with annoying clicks while chewing on a thin cocktail straw. Shaking his head, he threw his cards into the center, giving up.

They were at the turn; the dealer decisively flipped the card, revealing another seven. Telly looked up for direction, his hand hovering over the chips.

"Let's make this interesting. Toss in a hundred," Clutch ordered.

Telly fumbled with four green chips, sending the small column into an avalanche that spilled toward the center of the table, wincing when he heard Clutch call him a putz. Toupee man chirped, "Make it two." He rolled two black chips into the center of the table. Telly heard muttered curses and a soft grunt from the Asian man, who threw his cards into the muck with disgust. Hoodie boy rubbed two black chips between his fingers, shrugged, and tossed them toward the pot. "Call," he said lazily.

At this point, the hand was between him, hoodie kid, and toupee man, who was twisting the hair of his long sideburns. *Is the sideburn twisting good or bad?* Telly wondered. Clutch was quiet.

"That's right, Telly. We are playing poker. He thinks he got you. I see your eyes. Grandma drums her fingers when she's got nothing. Frick and Frack over here shuffle the cards exactly the same way, and Elvis is pulling at his facial hair like he's got trichotillomania."

Telly looked at the kid in the hoodie, a question in his face.

"Dotcom boy? He's an idiot; he has nothing. Don't worry about him. I can't see what the toupee is holding. He won't pick up his cards. Don't worry about me, Telly. I ain't worried."

Bully for you, Telly thought, swallowing hard. He picked at his bottom lip.

"Careful, partner. They're all watching for a message from you." Clutch was silent for a minute. "Let's get rid of the dotcom—go all in."

Toupee man threw in three hundred dollars, took a long pull on his drink, and burped gently. "Call," he added.

Dotcom's phone trilled. He glanced at the face, cursed, and threw away his cards. "I'll be back."

"Show him the boy," Clutch said to Telly, telling him to turn over his cards and reveal his jack.

Elvis stood, his toupee falling to the side of his head, covering his large ear. His face split into a crooked smile filled with tobacco-stained teeth. Crisply, he turned over a deuce-seven offsuit.

"Shit! Trips," Clutch muttered.

"Trips?" Telly squeaked, looking for support.

"Yeah," Toupee man sneered. "I got trip sevens; beat that, bozo."

Telly bit his lip furiously as the red blush of both anger and embarrassment stole over his face. He should never have trusted Clutch. He was playing blind. While he was busy studying the other players, he forgot to think about what they were holding. Clutch didn't know shit about the game either! Some big help he turned out to be.

"It ain't over, Telly; we got outs. We've still got the river, so don't cry me one yet," Clutch said with excitement.

All sound receded as the dealer placed the last card on the table. When his hand moved, Telly saw an eight of hearts. He felt a jolt and looked up to see Clutch, who was dancing on the table, his worn cowboy boots floating above the large pile of chips. "We did it! We did it!" he sang.

"Good river," Ramona called out. "Nicely played."

"Straight wins," the dealer announced to the table, pushing a mountain of chips totaling over two thousand dollars toward Telly.

"Sheeesh." The loser half stood to confirm his loss. "Luck doesn't last forever. He still doesn't get it. You won, jerk."

Ramona laughed deeply. "Straights always beat trips in my book. What's your name?"

"Telly Martin." He nodded politely to the older woman.

"Any relation to Dean?" The whole table stopped to look at him. "You know, Dean Martin, the Rat Pack?"

"No." Telly laughed. "I wish."

"I have to think of a name to call you," the old lady said. "Everybody's got to have a special name. You playing in the Series next week?"

Telly shook his head. "I don't know."

"I think you are. I'll see you there, and I'll have a name ready for you by then."

"Thanks," Telly said.

"Ramona Heart." She nodded to him. "I'm the Northeast Poker Champion. Anyone care to place a little wager this kid'll be there?"

Telly piled the chips in color-coordinated columns in front of him. He heard Clutch slap his hand together and say, "Like taking candy from a baby. I told you it was easy. Let's play some poker."

CHAPTER NINE

"I'll give you a ride home, Gretchen," said a voice behind her as she exited the building.

She waved him off. "No thanks, Rob."

The sun was lining the ridge of the mountains, separating light from dark.

"I insist." He pushed past her to open the door of his Firebird. "Hop in. I'm not going to bite you, Gretchen."

"Look, Rob, you know I'm with somebody."

Rob shrugged and said contemptuously, "Oh, the little guy."

"He's not little."

"He is to me." He revved his engine as if he were flexing his muscles.

"Not where it counts," she said contemptously. She looked at his face. His lips thinned, and he stuck his bottom lip out. She shouldn't have sparred with him.

"Come on, I'll give you a lift." Rob was persistent, his voice oily.

Gretchen shook her head. "I called a cab. It'll be here in a minute."

"Cancel it. You're making a big mistake here. I can make things real nice for you."

"What's that supposed to mean?" Gretchen asked angrily, feeling dreaded tears fill her eyes. She willed them not to fall.

"Don't come on Tuesday and see what it means," Rob said with a cruel twist to his thin mouth.

Gretchen sighed with relief when the cab pulled into the parking lot. She bit her fingernail to the quick, giving the driver the whole ten for a six-dollar ride without a thought. She headed up the concrete steps, her mind replaying her conversation with Rob, worried about what he was going to do. She didn't want to go back there, but they needed money to live. Telly had to get something going. She had wanted so badly for him to have the experience of his life, but it was too hot for her at work. She didn't feel safe anymore. Rob was a ticking time bomb, and she didn't want to get caught in his explosion. She nodded to Cheryl, who responded with a friendly greeting. She didn't want to talk, but it seemed she wasn't getting out without a few pleasantries.

They chatted about the weather, the lousy television reception, and the creep in 4A. Nobody was sure what he looked like, but they all knew his voice. He used it often enough to complain about the noise.

Cheryl turned to go in, paused, and said, "Oh, and Gretchen—please tell Telly he really doesn't have to pay us back."

Gretchen stopped, her face going numb, her hand on the doorknob. "What?"

"Yeah, Telly borrowed a few bucks from us tonight. Tell him we—"

"Telly borrowed...how much?"

"Five hundred, but—"

"Five hundred dollars?" Gretchen's voice rose.

"Yeah. He was so shy about it. But really. He's such a great...Gretchen?"

Gretchen ran into the room looking for Telly. She walked purposefully into the bedroom. The bed was fully made and empty. Sophie looked up from her little bed, snuffled, and went back to sleep.

"Telly?" she called out into the darkness, knowing she was alone...and pissed.

CHAPTER TEN

"I can't tell you how good this feels," Telly said, looking at the stacks of chips before him.

"Yeah, I'll bet," polyester man said sourly.

A crowd had developed on the balcony overlooking the poker room, all eyes on Telly's table.

"Quiet," Clutch told him. "Seat seven has an ace-king. Seat nine has pocket threes. Stop smirking, you idiot. What are you holding?" Telly felt the chill of Clutch behind him as he held open his hand for the ghost to see. "Pocket sixes. Raise."

"Raise," Telly repeated.

"Order a vodka," Clutch told him.

"Vodka? It's going on six in the morning."

"So get it with orange juice. Breakfast of champions."

"Drinks on Table 261!" the dealer called out. The pit boss motioned for a waitress to hurry over. A tall blond girl with impossibly long legs bent down to whisper, "What would you like?"

Telly shook his head, "No, thanks."

"Vodka and orange juice," Clutch whispered.

"I'm not in the mood," Telly said plainly.

"Uh-oh, here he goes again," toupee man whined. He had returned with more money. "Who do you think you are talking to?"

"How would you like it, sir?" the waitress persisted.

"Can we play here?" toupee man interrupted. He was beet red. Half of his sideburn was missing. "Get the drink and decide what you're doing!"

"Vodka, OJ, and reraise," Clutch advised.

Telly repeated the order.

The Asian man watched Telly and then said, "I raise one thousand."

The drink magically appeared at his elbow. "Give her a tip," Clutch told him. Telly picked up a five-dollar chip, heard Clutch growl at him, and went for a twenty-five-dollar one.

"You're up seventeen thousand dollars, man. Give her a hundred."

"A hundred?" Telly echoed.

"You have to match his thousand, not hundred," the dealer said impatiently.

Telly felt the cold sting of Clutch reach over to shove his hands onto the hundred-dollar chips.

"OK, OK already." He snatched a black chip and placed it on her water-marked tray.

"Thanks a lot," she said with a bright smile.

"Grandpappy always said, 'Give big, get big,'" Clutch said sagely.

Telly was tired; he wanted to go home. The thrill of the game had evaporated. There was a tenseness at the table that made his old job seem like a vacation. He sipped the icy drink, shuddering when the liquor painted his throat. He turned to the Asian man on his left. "How much do you have over there?"

"I have twenty-two thousand. Why?"

Telly looked at his pile of chips. He could walk out of here a big winner. He already had enough to pay Quick Daddy *and* get into the Series. He looked at the other man's pile thinking that he wanted to buy Gretchen something—something special. He finally got it. *Give big, get big.*

"I'm all in." He shoved all his money into the center of the table.

"That's what I'm talking about!" Clutch smiled.

The other player hesitated. His eyes searched Telly's face. Finally, he sighed and folded.

"What did you have?" the loser asked wearily.

"Tell him it's going to cost a hundred to see one card," Clutch said smugly.

Telly repeated the statement with a mumble.

"What did you say?" the Asian man questioned.

Telly looked at the faces surrounding him. They were all leaning forward, watching him, waiting expectantly. He was entertaining them. "I said it will cost you a hundred to see one card."

The man tossed a black chip, which circled Telly's obscene pile of money.

"Tell him to choose which one." Clutch was enjoying the evening immensely. *I could get used to this,* he thought happily. *Seems just like old times.*

There was a murmur of appreciation at the table. People were looking at him with respect and smiling with approval.

They were enjoying the show. Telly sat up straight, feeling incredibly cool. He finally had it—the cool factor. This was easy. "You pick it," he said boldly.

The other man pointed to the card on the right. Telly flipped it gently, exposing a six of hearts.

"You had a six?" The Asian man stood. "You went all in with a six?"

"You had nothing too," Telly accused.

The table got very silent.

"How did you know I had nothing?"

"Careful, Telly," Clutch warned him.

"I…I…"

"You read his tell!" Clutch shouted.

"I read your tell."

"The hell you did." The player stood and put on his jacket, a look of disgust on his face.

"He won. Fair and square," Ramona said. She'd stopped playing hours before but had stayed to watch the game. "He's a strange little bugger, but he won fair and square."

"Drinks all around." Telly placed another hundred-dollar chip on the waitress's tray. "I'm heading home."

"What?" Clutch crouched next to Telly, who was busy stacking his chips into a tray. "I'm just getting started."

Telly shook his head. "Nope, I'm done."

"Played a good hand," Ramona nodded sagely.

"I'm tired," Telly said to the table. He tipped the dealer three hundred dollars. The dealer nodded with surprise.

"Wise decision," she agreed. "Not smart to play when you're tired. I'm still thinking on a name to call you. You playing here tomorrow?"

Telly shook his head. "Probably not."

"Like hell you say," Clutch said angrily.

Telly grinned at Clutch as he carried the four trays of chips toward the cashier. Clutch steamed with frustrated rage. Telly refused to let it bring him down or allow Clutch to bully him anymore. He was tired.

"I want to thank you," Telly said with astonishment at the two stacks of ten thousand dollars, plus a few thousand extra. Just yesterday morning he would have given his eye teeth to hold a couple thousand, and here he was tipping hundred chips like they were nickels and dimes.

"You're so welcome, sir," the cashier smiled back. Telly plucked out a hundred-dollar bill and handed it to her. "Thank you." She nodded, folding it in half and sliding it into her pocket. He could get used to this, he thought, feeling great.

"Very nice," Clutch said sarcastically. "If you keep tipping like that, you'll go through all your money in no time."

"You said, 'Give big, get big.'" Telly shrugged, pushing up his glasses, which had slid down his nose.

"You can't give big if you don't play enough."

"Look," Telly said, "it's six thirty in the morning." People gave him a wide berth. He realized that he was getting some strange looks. "Come on." He motioned toward the entrance. "I have to get home and tell Gretchen," he whispered, his eyes darting around. He realized suddenly that he was alone.

CHAPTER ELEVEN

Clutch found himself outside his former home, noticing a shutter hung off one of the windows. The large flowerpots that Ginny had always filled with flowers stood barren, the dirt dry and cracked. Clutch walked through the door, surprised at the threadbare rug. He didn't remember it being so worn. Ginny lay curled on her side on the sagging couch, her plump hand under her puffy cheek. A bottle of something was on the lamp table. Clutch picked it up. *Tequila?* Ginny never drank. Her pursed lips blew gently. Clutch knelt beside her, his ghostly fingers stroking her graying hair from her sweaty face. New lines bracketed her mouth. She wet her lips, a tear leaking from her closed eye. "Clutch," she sighed.

The ring of the phone broke the silence of the room. Ginny rose, bleary-eyed, to answer it. She rubbed her face with a weary hand. "I got them," she said softly. She staggered to a table with a pile of mail, the phone close to her ear, and held up plane tickets to Phoenix. "I know. I know. But I can't." The other person spoke for a long time. She wiped a tear from her eye. "I told you, I'm sorry, but…I'm not ready. I'm really sorry." The line went dead.

Clutch looked at the lone plant, which was wilting in the Vegas heat. His normally tidy and clean home looked unkempt, as did Ginny. She had always been so happy, filled with sunshine. She looked so…alone now. He didn't like to think about that. They had been together ten years; she was considerably younger, and he'd never given a thought to the fact that he might leave her completely and utterly alone. She had no one to watch over her.

His mind raced as he saw scene after scene from the ten years they were together. She worked hard, bringing in money when he didn't. She watched his kid on the days Ruby stayed with them. He had to work—sometimes games went for days—but Ginny never complained. Not like Jenny, the bitch he'd married. Pursing his lip, he tried to remember if he'd ever thanked her. Nothing came to mind. He should have told her he loved her. He wished he had said it at least once. He bent over to kiss the powdery skin of her cheek.

"Tell her now," Sten, the avenging angel, said from behind him.

Clutch stood, his face a mask of hatred. "What are you doing here?" he demanded.

Sten ignored him. He gestured to the woman staring out the back door to the overgrown yard. "She'll be happy to hear it. Say it."

Clutch launched himself at the levitating man, but their forms merely passed through each other, doing no harm. He landed in a heap, smashing against the fireplace. Above him, an urn wobbled from its perch on the mantle. Clutch watched as it wavered. Sten held out a hand to catch it, but Clutch leaped up, knocking it from the white hands, letting it fall onto the swirling patterns of the braided rug. “I don’t need your help!” he shouted.

The urn lay on the floor, its top rolling under a chair, gray dust puffing out.

Ginny jumped at the disturbance, but all she saw was Clutch’s urn lying on the floor. She figured it must have tipped from its spot. She knew she should have put it in a safer place. She bent down and collected the container, holding it close to her chest. “I still miss him,” she moaned. “I can’t, Stan. I can’t.”

“Stan?” Clutch whispered, not knowing who she was talking about.

“Everybody needs help at one time or another,” Sten said as he winked out of the room.

Clutch stared at his Ginny holding what was left of his cremains. “Not if they don’t exist,” he replied to nobody in particular. He faded out of the room.

CHAPTER TWELVE

Telly opened the door to his apartment as quietly as he could. Closing the door with equal care, he failed to see Gretchen on the orange sofa, her face set with anger.

"Telly Martin," she whispered harshly, "it's seven o'clock in the morning."

Startled, Telly dropped the cash he was taking out of his pocket. It fell on the floor, coming out of its strap and spreading in a wide arc from his feet. Gretchen jumped up, gasping. Sophie the belly-dancing dog ran in circles around the money, wheezing. *Oh, this you notice,* he thought, looking at the excited dog.

"Where did you get all that money!" she demanded.

Telly pulled out a packet of ten thousand from each side of his pants, thrusting it into Gretchen's hand. They both bent to pick up the cash from the floor. Gretchen stacked it carelessly on the coffee table.

"I won it, Gretch," he told her excitedly.

Narrowing her bright eyes, she looked at him skeptically.

"Really. I did."

"You hit a jackpot? In a machine?"

"Poker. I won it all at poker."

"How? How could you have played, Telly? You didn't have anything to join a game."

Sophie decided to bark loudly at that moment, and the man from 4A banged against the wall. "Loser…I'm sick and tired of your noise. I'm gonna come there and throw that dog out the window," he called again.

Telly lowered his head, mumbling, "Quick Daddy and Cheryl…"

"You took money from Cheryl…?"

"Borrowed. Listen, I can explain everything," Telly said urgently.

Clutch appeared next to Gretchen and interrupted. "Don't do it, Telly."

"Oh, now you're back?" Telly spat to Clutch.

"I've been here for hours," Gretchen answered hotly.

"She's pissed." Clutch laughed.

"Shut up!" Telly told Clutch rudely.

"What?" Gretchen said with shock. Tears leaked down her face and made her mascara run.

Telly turned to her. "Not you, Gretchen."

Clutch grabbed his arm. "She'll never believe you, pal. You're gonna ruin everything."

"I told you to leave me alone," Telly yelled at Clutch, batting his arms wildly.

Gretchen stood, fury and hurt making her vibrate. "Leave you alone? Maybe I should."

"Gretch, not you. Him," Telly said, pointing to empty air.

Gretchen looked, her hands wiping her tears. "I don't know what you are talking about."

"I won tonight. I won big, but I won with…a little help."

"What?"

"Clutch…Clutch Henderson helped me."

Gretchen rolled her eyes impatiently. She tapped her foot, her hands on her hips. "That is the stupidest thing I've ever heard. Clutch Henderson—really? What, did you take his book to the tables and cheat?" She grabbed his hands palms up. "Did you write crib notes on your hands?"

Telly pulled his hands away, his face suffused with red.

Gretchen felt anger building in her chest until she felt the walls caving in. Sweet, dependable Telly had ignored everything they'd discussed. He was treating her like a...a... nothing. Her job was hanging by a thread. Words failed her. She didn't want to tell him about Rob. She didn't want to add more to his shoulders and tell him about the other thing. Not yet. She never complained…never. "Didn't we decide you weren't going to play anymore, Telly? What happened to your responsibility to me?"

Telly watched in mute shock as Gretchen's anger became a living thing. They hardly ever fought. He followed her as she stalked to the bedroom. "We talked it over. You were going for a job. The experiment ended. You agreed to stop." She covered her face with her hands forlornly. "You are putting me in a bad situation."

"Aren't you being a little melodramatic?"

"Uh-oh, that was stupid," Clutch remarked.

"Do me a favor and don't help me," Telly yelled at Clutch.

"Don't help you? You don't appreciate anything I've done," Gretchen cried.

"No, Gretchen." Telly followed, trying to get her to calm down. "He's here. He didn't give me a choice. He keeps talking to me."

"I don't believe this," Gretchen said.

"Told ya," Clutch added from his spot by the doorframe.

Telly spun, pointing his finger. "I told you to stay out of this."

Gretchen watched, her eyes widening as Telly spoke to the air. "Don't talk to me that way!"

"I wasn't talking to you. I was talking to him!" Telly pointed to a darkened corner of the room.

"That was dumb," Clutch told him. "She can't see me."

"Why me? Why am I the only one that sees you?" Telly turned to Gretchen and pleaded, "Look hard, Gretch. Can't you see him?"

Clutch shrugged, but Gretchen rounded on Telly, her temper up. "Who…what are you talking about? There's nobody here but us."

"Clutch Henderson is in the room."

Gretchen's eyes filled with both anger and frustration. "No, Telly. There's nobody here."

Telly took her hand, which she pulled away, annoyed at him. "I spent the evening with Clutch Henderson. He went with me to play poker. He's helping me."

"That guy died. It was in all the papers and all over the news. He's been dead for a year now."

"I know," Telly calmly agreed, leading her to the foot of the bed, where they sat on the edge. "He's a ghost."

"Telly, please don't make up stories."

Telly stood to pace the room. "I have never lied to you. He's here, right now, leaning against the doorframe." He looked hard at Clutch. "He's laughing at us."

Gretchen shook her head. "Stop it. Stop it right now. You're scaring me."

"Oh, don't be scared," Telly said, misunderstanding her meaning. "He's not a scary ghost." Telly spoke urgently, trying to make her understand. "I mean, he was a little scary to me at first, but then—"

"OK. I think I've had enough. I have to think. Look, we made a pact. A couple of weeks and then you would stop." Gretchen was at the end of her rope.

"I made money tonight. That was part of the pact, too. We're just getting started."

"It's dirty money. I don't know how, but it's dirty. It's not enough to live on for long. Haven't you realized that already? There is no future in this."

"There's twenty thousand dollars on that coffee table." Telly pointed to the other room.

"Haven't you learned from the last time you won? It doesn't last. It's not steady," Gretchen argued.

"I did steady for twelve years, and where did that get me?"

"Don't start, Telly. Once we pay the rent, living expenses, and such, you'll need some for another game."

Gretchen paced the room, ticking off her points on her fingers. "Then when you lose that, you'll need some more." She turned to face him, her voice imploring, "Don't you see, Telly, with gambling, there is never enough. Things are changing!" Gretchen cried out.

"What's changing? Nothing's changed between us. But I won. What if I win again, and again?"

Gretchen raised her eyebrow. Her arms were folded. Telly had never seen her so intractable.

"It could happen." Telly shrugged.

"I only agreed to this whole plan because you were so depressed about not finding a job." She continued more to herself: "I wanted you to have some fun, you know? Get it out of your system. But now I want my steady old Telly back," she whined.

"Steady old Telly," he repeated with disgust.

"I didn't mean it the way it sounded."

"Well, it sounded shitty. Like I'm some sort of pet."

She stood and pointed at Telly's chest. "You know what? You are having a nervous breakdown. Poker is messing with your mind. You're twisting everything I say. I don't think I can deal with this right now. I have enough to worry about. Oh…I don't know what to do. I have to think of how to handle this…"—she turned to look at him—"…how to handle you." She went to the closet and pulled out an overnight bag. She threw a few things haphazardly into the bag.

Telly was panicked. "Stop, Gretch. What are you doing?" He grabbed the handle of her bag to try to stop her.

"Let her go, Telly." Clutch struggled with Telly. "Chicks like her are a dime a dozen. My grandpappy always said, 'Don't chase after a woman or a bus. There'll always be another one.'"

"Leave; get out of here!" Telly slapped at the air, and his glasses flew off his head.

Gretchen stared at him, her blue eyes widening. "You told me to stop you. It's like you're possessed."

"You don't know the half of it," Telly said.

"I feel like I don't know you," Gretchen sobbed loudly. She stormed from the room, her bag under one arm. She scooped up Sophie and headed out the door. "This isn't a dream come true; it's a nightmare."

"Gretchen!" Telly yelled, moving to go after her. Sophie turned, her baleful, crooked eyes watching mournfully.

The phone cord traveled from the side of the bed, wrapping itself around Telly's ankles. He went down like a stone, flat on his face.

"Let her cool off. You're not gonna get anywhere. She's just pissed off at you right now," Clutch said amicably.

Telly tore off the cord clumsily and rose to take off after her. Gretchen was outside getting into a cab.

"Gretchen!" He called after her, tripping down the steps. "Gretch..." He stood in the empty street, watching the cab disappear. "She doesn't have any money. She has no place to go," he said sadly. "Thick and thin," he whispered, his heart breaking.

"It's like Buster said, 'Don't chase after women or buses.'"

Telly looked at Clutch. "You did this. I hate you."

"Hate's a strong word, son."

"Well, I feel strongly that I hate you. Leave me alone." Telly stomped up the steps to return dejectedly back to his apartment.

"There's two ways to look at this."

Telly jumped, realizing he was not alone. "I told you to leave."

"We could do this the hard way, or the easy way," Clutch told him.

"Or no way. I'm finished. The only person I care about is not here. I'm going to get a job."

"She's gone, buddy. You don't have to do that anymore."

Telly didn't answer. He grabbed his glasses, scooped up a few bucks from the pile on the table, abandoned the rest, and slammed the door, Clutch hot on his heels. Neither of them noticed that the door jammed, bounced, and swung wide open, revealing the pile of cash in his living room to anyone passing by.

CHAPTER THIRTEEN

Telly called Gretchen's number six times, and each time it went straight to voice mail.

His hands shoved into his pockets, he walked the streets for hours, ending up three miles away at Gretchen's friend and coworker, Chrissy's, place. The street grew busy and school buses made their stops, but Telly stood in the lee of the house waiting for the morning to progress before he knocked on the door. His stomach rumbled, but he refused to go to the McDonald's around the corner for fear of missing an opportunity to see if Gretchen was there.

"She's not there," a voice said from his left, startling him.

Telly glanced sideways to see Clutch sitting on the curb next to him. "I told you to leave me alone."

Clutch shook his head. "Can't." He threw a coin in the air, causing Telly to look up. The coin pulled at Telly's chest, twisting what was left of his heart. "We're connected, you and me. I can't leave, and now you can't either. We have a job to do."

"Well," Telly said leaning backward against a street sign, "you can't make me."

"I don't have to."

* * *

Chrissy emerged from her home, wrapping a robe around her trim figure.

"Well, hello mama…" Clutch drawled.

"Telly, what are you doing here?" she demanded.

"Is Gretchen in there with you?"

"Gretchen? No, Telly, she's not. Why?" Crissy said nastily.

"Told you," Clutch said with satisfaction.

"Shut up," Telly told him.

"You shut up. You're such a loser, Telly. I told Gretchen she was wasting her time with you. At least with Rob she might have a future."

"Rob?" Telly exploded. "She's with Rob Couts?"

Chrissy shrugged. "Maybe. I don't know. He likes her. Thinks she's pretty." Chrissy sniffled. "He asked her to come to his house party. He plays poker…a lot. And *wins*." Then she added defensively, "He invited me too."

Telly anxiously paced the street, his hands pulling at his unkempt hair. "What day?"

"I'm not sure," Chrissy lied. "You were supposed to get a job so you could help her today. It's eight o'clock; why are you still here?"

"What do you mean she's going to a party at his house? Gretchen would never do that."

"He's interested in her, and he let her know it. He can give her a better life than you. You haven't brought in much of anything for months."

"Gretchen's not interested in him," Telly persisted.

"You don't know that," Chrissy said snidely. "All a girl wants is to be taken care of by her man. You haven't done much of that lately."

"It's not like that with us."

Chrissy sniffled, "If you say so, but meanwhile you're the one out looking for her at eight in the morning."

"Shit, it's eight already?"

"Time flies when you're having fun," Clutch laughed.

"I'm not having fun," Telly growled.

"Neither is she," Chrissy sneered. "Weren't you supposed to be at a job interview this morning?" Chrissy looked at him skeptically.

"Where is she?" Telly demanded.

"I told you I don't know. You better leave here or I'm calling the cops." Telly opened his mouth, shutting it when she said firmly, "I mean it, Telly." She showed him the pink iPhone in the palm of her hand.

Telly reeled backward. He had no idea where else she might have gone. He called Gretchen's mother's number, but when the phone rang, he hung up. He didn't like Maggie, and she hated him. She'd never go there and hear that her mother was right after all. *What about Rob Couts?* he thought. She wouldn't have. That's why she was so upset; poor Gretch. Her boss was hitting on her, and she didn't feel comfortable. She was right about the money, though, he admitted. The last time he'd won, they'd lived on it for a short while, but he'd needed the bulk of it to finance new games. It was never going to work; he slapped himself on the forehead. He cursed himself for being both thoughtless and selfish. Why didn't she tell him? He would make it up to her. He would beg for a cab job, but he was too punch-drunk to go now. He needed to shut his eyes for a few minutes. He headed home.

He set his phone's alarm for two hours later. Telly didn't remember falling into his bed or even covering himself. He didn't notice that the money he'd left on the table was gone. Exhausted, his mind numb with hurt, he sank into a deep slumber, unaware that Clutch sat on the end of the bed, watching and waiting.

Telly snored, and his eyes sunk into his head. Clutch covered him with the fluffy comforter and sat watching the kid sleep. He walked out to look for the cash. Sten materialized on the rusty-orange couch.

"The guy from 4A took it," Sten told him.

"Crap, we'll have to start all over." He looked at Sten. "How'd that happen?"

"Telly left the door unlocked. He passed by, saw it, and took it."

"That stupid ass. I ought to—"

"Haven't you done enough? Your daughter's been robbed; your wife and girlfriend are fighting over your winnings. The love of his life has walked out on him. She's on the verge of being taken advantage of because she's afraid to lose their only income."

"Do you know where she went?" Clutch demanded.

Sten inclined his head.

"Do you?"

"You want me to do everything? What will you learn if I do? I don't know, Clutch. That bracelet looks farther and farther away. Maybe you should set your sights on something more attainable. Maybe your grandfather was right and you really are a loser." Sten's voice was laced with contempt.

Clutch swung drunkenly, but Sten easily outmaneuvered him. "You don't know anything about Buster and me!" he shouted. He stood nose to nose with Sten, and the angel floated, surrounded by a rainbow of colors that tingled against Clutch's skin. He pointed to the fluorescent white shirt. "That bracelet is mine! Nobody is going to stand in the way of my win." He paused for a minute. "Wait, what do you mean my daughter's been robbed? Is she OK?"

"About time you thought about someone other than yourself. Is she OK? That depends on your point of view," Sten answered as he let himself fade.

"What a crock of shit!" he shouted at the waning image of the sentinel. "Come back here, you interfering know-it-all!"

While he waited for Telly to get up, the angel's words rankled him. Time ticked by, and Clutch had to admit that watching Telly sleep was more boring than watching him play poker. He decided to take a stroll.

CHAPTER FOURTEEN

It was weird. The street had that familiar look, yet it felt foreign and small, like a kid's playset. They'd had a pretty big house in their day, during the glory years. He was playing the poker circuit, winning big money. Jenny and his kid had a nice little setup on the north side of town. It was a big house back then, but now it seemed run-down, just short of shabby. The stucco was cracked; bird droppings plastered the tiled roof. The window in their entry had a crack in the corner that had somehow never gotten fixed, and the aluminum had turned black and moldy-looking. Jenny'd let the lawn go, and instead of the green oasis he had paid for, there was a field of dusty gravel, weeds poking through in clumpy knots.

The sidewalk was jagged, the driveway a mess—Clutch wondered what the hell she had done with his winnings. The living room was dark, the olive shag carpet spotted with pet stains. "Damn dog," he cursed. He looked around but couldn't see an animal anywhere.

Jenny was sprawled across the couch, her feet dangling off the end. She had put on weight, Clutch noticed. An ashtray overflowing with butts, a half-empty bottle of

Southern Comfort, and crumpled magazines littered the scarred coffee table.

Clutch wandered around the room, his fingers stirring the dust, stopping when he came to a picture of Ruby. It was her third- or fourth-grade class picture in a cardboard frame that warped slightly. The picture had faded over time; his daughter's face looked sallow from exposure to cigarette smoke. Picking it up, he smiled at his daughter's sweet, tomboyish smile. She looked like him, only pretty. His calloused finger touched the apple of her cheek, her blue eyes knowing, even at eight. Her ash-blond hair was in a sideways ponytail that he might have even made for her that day, or maybe not. It didn't matter much anyway. Clutch sighed. Who remembered that stuff, anyway?

Jenny coughed deeply. She was sitting up, staring right at him, her face sour. Clutch turned to look at her and realized that she didn't see him. She was fully dressed in a sleeveless shirt and rumpled black pants. Reaching down, she picked up the half-empty glass and took a quick swallow.

Oh yeah, he thought. *That's why.* She hadn't kicked him out, he remembered. He'd left.

"Ruby," she called loudly, her voice a rusty scrape. "Move your ass. It's going on ten, and I have to get to the lawyers." She pulled herself unsteadily to her feet. "Lazy piece of…Ruby, I ain't got all day."

Clutch's eyes followed her as she left the room, anticipation building at the sounds of his daughter getting ready.

"Ruby!" she called again.

"I heard you," Ruby called back. It was a woman's voice, not a child's. Clutch walked to the stairs, his foot on the bottom rung. If he'd had a heart it would've been beating furiously in his chest. It felt like ages since he'd seen her. She was an adult now—almost seventeen. Divorce had made her grow up fast. That, and the twenty-seven-year-old she had hooked up with. He hated Roy with a passion that bordered on insanity.

Ruby appeared at the top of the stairs, her hair an interesting shade of blue, her light eyes ringed with dark circles. Her skin was so white, it was translucent. She wore some kind of black spandex shorts with ripped denim over them. Her top was a Band-Aid with spaghetti straps, her bared shoulders covered with colorful tattoos. She was wearing short dark boots and a ring in her nose that connected to her earring with a chain.

Clutch swallowed convulsively, looking at the alien that was his daughter. He hoped she wasn't still involved with that creep, Roy. He was a bad dude. He glanced behind her, satisfied that no one was following. Clutch came close, looking at her eyes. At least they looked normal.

She looked like a homeless person. He shook his head. He should have taken his kid when he'd left. He tried to remember why he didn't. His occupation didn't jibe well with family life. He couldn't do the whole picket fence thing. He lived on a reverse schedule. He needed to sleep during the day and made his living at night.

"I told you to wake me," Jenny said.

Ruby sniffed. "Your screaming kept me up all night."

"I wasn't screaming; I was talking to your father's slut."

Ruby shrugged indifferently. "I don't know why you insist on fighting with Daddy's girlfriend."

Clutch's ears pricked up—Ginny and Jenny in a fight?

"I didn't start it; she did," Jenny spat. "Three weeks after Clutch died, that bitch filed a lawsuit for the money. There was no will; her fancy lawyer claimed we were married on paper only."

"They were as good as married," Ruby pointed out. "Dad loved her. I know he did."

"Clutch didn't know the meaning of that word. You always gave him more credit than he deserved. He was the most self-serving bastard that ever lived," Jenny spat.

Somewhere in the region of Clutch's chest, a small spark stirred, making his shriveled heart protest with the abuse from his ex.

Jenny dismissed her daughter with a wave of her hand as she disappeared into the downstairs bathroom. "Screw her and you too," she added maliciously.

Ruby threw herself onto the couch. "She's really OK, and she needs the money."

"So do we," came the curt reply.

"You could split it. That way, we all get some of it." Ruby got up to go into the kitchen. She pulled out a skillet. "I'm making eggs; you want some?" she called out. No response. Ruby took out a few stalks of asparagus, cutting them into small pieces; then she added a neat pile of tiny, perfectly chopped chives. Clutch admired her knife skills.

She whipped eggs, put in a pinch of salt, and expertly flipped her omelet. Clutch clapped with stunned appreciation. Ruby paused, looking around the filthy kitchen, her eyes weary.

Where did she learn that? he wondered. Pulling out a stool, she sat at the counter eating her eggs while leafing through a brochure.

"All you're doing is making the lawyers richer," she said without looking up as her freshly showered mother entered the room. Clutch looked at her. He noticed that she cleaned up nicely, but he still didn't like her. Jenny was mean.

"She's not getting anything."

"That's not what my father wanted."

"Then he should have been responsible and made a will." Jenny made a cup of black coffee. "He left us high and dry."

"He paid the support until he died."

Jenny gave her a dirty look.

"Well, he tried. He hit a bad patch; you can't blame him for that."

"Good girl." Clutch came up behind her. Ruby shivered, a chill going through her slender body.

"Yeah, he was father of the year. I'm not sharing his winnings. Anyway, why do you care about Clutch's bimbo?"

"She was always nice to me, even when Dad stopped talking to me."

Jenny made a rude noise and said, "Oliver Henderson owes me."

Clutch winced when she said his real name. Nobody ever called him that except for Jenny. He hated her even more for that.

"If you don't stop this senseless battle over the money, there will be nothing left," Ruby told her, pointing her fork at her to stress her words.

Jenny eyed her daughter. She had given her nothing but trouble since she'd hit puberty. She was a daddy's girl, and when Clutch stopped talking to her over that guy, she thought their relationship wouldn't be able to be fixed—and it wasn't, in spite of all the times that Ginny called and tried to make it better. *Interfering bitch,* she thought. "If you like her so much, why don't you go and stay with her? Let *her* pay your way."

Ruby looked up, her eyes sparking with hostility. "Don't think she hasn't offered."

"All you care about is that stupid cooking school. Trust me, you're not even that good."

"At least she's offered to help with my tuition." Ruby closed the brochure she was looking at. "Ginny says Dad would've wanted me to go."

"He didn't speak to you for a year!"

"It was my fault." Ruby stood next to the trash, dropping the folder into the pail. "He was trying to teach me something."

"All your father cared about was the game. Not you, or me, or even that woman—"

"Ginny," Ruby said helpfully. "None of this is her fault. She didn't break up your marriage."

"She helped," Jenny sneered through her teeth.

Ruby laughed contemptuously. "Believe me, Mom. You didn't need any help."

Jenny reached across the counter and slapped Ruby across the face. "It's a short ride from here to the homeless shelter."

"Homeless shelter?" Clutch said out loud. Both women stopped, looking around the room. Somehow it broke the tension.

"My rules, remember? You don't have Clutch to run to anymore."

"I didn't run to him the last time," Ruby said softly.

"That's because he wouldn't talk to you while you dated that junkie."

"We broke up."

Jenny grunted as she poured her coffee into the sink. "You didn't break up. He went to jail."

"Jail, humph. Good," Clutch said with a smile. He hated that guy.

"None of that matters. I'm clean now. I wish Dad could see that."

"He was so busy with his life, he didn't know you ruined your own."

"You know that's not true."

"What did he ever do for you?" Jenny demanded. "Oh, I don't have time for this! He didn't sit up with you at night; I did. He do homework? Make you dinner? Don't think so—he did nothing. The best thing he ever did was drop dead so I could finally get my share...the one I deserve." She threw her hands in the air. "What's the use? It's my money. I'll see it burn before she gets it."

"Those men who came, the ones that Daddy owed…"

"Fuck them. Let them go to Clutch to collect."

"It wasn't his fault either," Ruby said to Jenny's back as they walked out of the house. "He refused to speak to me when I quit school."

Jenny spun, her face a mask of hatred. "He should have been here. Nobody is getting that money but me." She pointed to her chest, another one he'd paid for. "I've been robbed!" she shouted.

Ah, Clutch thought, the lightbulb going off in his head. *That's what Sten meant.* "No, Ruby's been robbed—her future stolen from her," Clutch said to himself.

"That home wrecker will get nothing, I swear. She won't see a penny, unless it's over my dead body," she swore.

"That could be arranged." Clutch surged forward but felt himself being held back in a merciless grip. "Let me go!" he screamed at Sten. "This is my house!"

The sentinel had a habit of showing up and interfering with Clutch's plans.

"Not anymore, Clutch. This isn't your fight. It's theirs. You deserted this boxing ring years ago."

"I didn't desert them. I was trying to make a living."

"If you start to believe your own bullshit, Clutch, you'll never get anywhere," Sten laughed.

"It's true!" Clutch responded.

The door slammed. The women and Sten were gone. Clutch walked into the kitchen, fishing out the pamphlet that had held his daughter's interest. It was an application to the Culinary School of Nevada. Ruby had ambition; he felt stirrings of pride. He'd always said she was a smart kid. Took after him. He tucked it under his arm and left.

CHAPTER FIFTEEN

Telly rubbed the beard from his bleary face. Putting on the Vince shirt Gretchen had bought him for Christmas, he slipped on his shoes and walked into the living area. He pulled his wallet and a small wad of cash from his pocket. Looking down at the coffee table, he noticed that the money was gone. His heart started to race. He dropped to his knees and crawled around on the floor, lifting the skirt of the couch to search underneath it. Frantically, he moved his hands on the matted carpet, cursing under his breath when he found nothing. His mouth went dry. Had he dreamt the whole thing? No, Gretchen was gone, and he still had about seven hundred dollars. He pulled out five hundred and left. As he walked past Cheryl's apartment, he quietly slipped it under the door.

He grabbed a bus on Maryland Parkway, getting off a block from George's Cab Service.

"You scored a perfect one hundred on the test, Telly. You're lucky you came in today," George told him as he handed over a stack of papers.

"Really, why?" Lucky was a word Telly never used to describe himself.

"Starting next week, all drivers have to be approved by the NTA. You would lose a week waiting for the approval to go through. We got a fight tomorrow, and I have to fill the vehicles. If you want, you can start tonight."

"What time?"

"Be back at six."

Telly nodded and walked out into the bright Vegas sun. Squinting, he dialed Gretchen's cell, hanging up when it went to voice mail. He grabbed a bus on Industrial heading toward Summerlin.

An hour later, he got off on Decatur and stopped at Starbucks to buy three coffees. Then he walked the five blocks to his parents' home.

They lived in a neat subdivision in a four-bedroom house built in the late nineties. It was in a gated community with scores of identical khaki-painted stucco homes built so closely together they almost touched. The moderately affluent area was mostly inhabited by transplants from other states here for retirement. His parents were former teachers who had bought into the inexpensive Vegas lifestyle after living and struggling to make ends meet in Los Angeles.

"Mom!" he called out after letting himself in. He heard whispered voices and a door slamming in the rear of the house. "Mom? Dad?"

Harriet Martin came into the room wearing a raspberry-pink Juicy velour tracksuit. "Telly!" she cooed, her arms outstretched. "What brings you to this side of town?"

He leaned forward to kiss her cheek, handing her the cardboard tray of coffee. "I was in the neighborhood and figured I'd check in. Where's Dad?"

"He'll be right back; he went to the market." She eyed the kitchen nervously. Telly looked at his mother. She was a tad too loud, her face flushed, her eyes darting to the other room.

"Is everything OK, Mom?" He looked toward the kitchen alcove.

Harriet put her arm around his shoulders. "What could be wrong now that you're here? Come, sit, tell me what's new in your life."

"Don't you want to go into the kitchen?"

She laughed. "No, let's sit right here on the new couch and have our coffee."

"You want to sit here?" Telly asked incredulously. Harriet was a maniac about cleaning. She never even let him wear shoes in the house. He looked at her pinkish-white hair, frozen in an upswept pompadour, and her fuchsia-colored nails. *Nothing new there,* he thought.

She sat gingerly on the edge of the sofa. As Telly sat, he put his cup on the glass surface of the coffee table without a coaster. "Telly!" she yelled.

"If you don't want to be in here, we could go into the kitchen and drink at the counter like normal people."

She waved her hand. "Never mind. It's OK. Just be careful of the carpet."

"Where's Mannix?" he asked. His big brother lived with his parents. He also had a sister named Gidget who was a grade school teacher in Florida. Some people named their children for family members; his parents named them after television characters. In Telly's opinion, this was not one of their more endearing traits.

"He's back in Los Angeles for a commercial. It's a small part, but the money was good." Mannix was an actor of dubious talent. "So?" Harriet sipped her coffee, her brown eyes unblinking in her face. She was making him nervous.

Telly watched her suspiciously. She didn't ask about working or even about Gretchen. Something was off. His father opened the front door, his fanny pack in his hand and his face red and sweaty, as though he had just finished running a race. He was wiping his forehead with a wilted linen handkerchief.

"Will you look who's here? Telly!" he shouted.

"I thought Mom said you went to the market."

"I did; I'm coming home now."

"Why didn't you come in through the garage?" Telly asked suspiciously.

"I walked," Frank Martin replied hurriedly.

"In this heat?" Telly asked.

"The sweating is good for you," Harriet interjected.

"Detoxing. Very important when you reach our age, right, Har?"

Telly looked at their faces, trying to figure out what was going on. His father sat down and took the proffered cup. "What's new, kiddo?"

"You guys OK?"

"Never better; what's going on?" Frank dismissed Telly's concern with a wave of his hand.

"I just wanted to let you know that...well, I've decided to take a job at a cab service...for now. Until something better comes along."

Harriet clapped her hands. "That's wonderful!" She stood, looked at the kitchen, and said, "Oh! I just realized I left something on the stove. Let me go grab it." Not the reaction he was expecting. They had been psychotic when he'd decided to try his hand at gambling. The expectations were always high and nonnegotiable. The fact they were so pleased with a cab-driving job in itself didn't make any sense. Harriet fled the room. Telly noticed she had Juicy Couture printed in gothic, silver letters across the wide expanse of her butt.

"What's she cooking?" he asked.

"Soup, oatmeal...who knows? Tell me, Telly, what happened to the poker?"

Telly looked at his father's earnest face. He still had most of his hair, and oddly enough it had never grayed. He wore heavy tortoiseshell glasses and had a very neat mustache under his long nose. With his bushy black brows, he looked like he was wearing a Groucho Marx trick nose and glasses.

"Well, is it soup or oatmeal?" Telly stood to go into the kitchen.

"Who cares? Tell me what's new in your life." His father grabbed his arm, pulling him back to the couch. *Something was going on*, Telly knew it.

"You asked that already. Dad, what's going on?"

"Nothing...not a thing. You were telling me about the driving job."

"Poker wasn't working out, so I took the cab job temporarily."

"You'll get something in computers. You're the best. This is only a setback." His father assured him.

"It wasn't a setback; it was a disaster."

"You could go back to school. Get a business degree."

"And waste another hundred thousand and four years, hey—don't you want to ask about Gretchen?" Telly looked at his father suspiciously.

"Gretchen?" His father looked startled. "I always want to know about Gretchen. I love Gretchen," he said loudly.

"What's going on here?" Telly got up and stalked into the kitchen. His mother was coming in from the back door. "Who's staying in the casita?" He walked to the rear window to look at the small one-bedroom apartment that was attached to the house. The blinds were pulled down, and he could see that the lights were on. He put his hand on the doorknob, and his mother stopped him.

"No! Don't go in there. It's a mess," she shrieked.

"Mom?" Telly said, his voice rising.

Harriet pulled up a kitchen chair, her face deflated. "Don't go out there. I promised I wouldn't tell."

"Wouldn't tell what?"

"Gretchen asked us not to say she was here," she blurted.

"Gretchen is here?" Relief bloomed in Telly's chest.

"Where else did you expect her to go?" Harriet said. "She loves you and needed to be with other people who love you. You weren't very nice to her. Sounds to me like things got pretty out of hand." She had a way of making him feel like a four-year-old. "I understand you are under a lot of pressure, but I never expected to hear such terrible things from your mouth."

"People fight. We had a disagreement." Telly felt himself shrinking under his mother's scrutiny. *Why did I stop here?* he wondered, not for the first time.

"Sounds to me like it was a little more than that."

"The gambling is not right for you. It's not what we sent you to college for. Besides, if you needed money, you should have come to us and not that…that pimp," his father said gravely. "You could stay in the casita instead of paying rent in that roach motel."

"Thanks, Dad. But the casita is Manny's space."

"You could stay in my craft room for a a while, until you..."

"Thanks, but no thanks. Is she in there now? I want to talk to her."

Harriet shrugged. "Well, I don't know—"

Telly ignored her and opened the door, heading purposefully to the little cottage. He stepped carefully on the gravel path, trying to make as little noise as possible. He tapped on the window.

"Gretch—open up. We need to talk." He heard Sophie's frantic barking.

The blinds parted, and Telly saw Gretchen's worried eyes through the small opening.

"Come on, Gretchen. I need to speak to you." He knocked again and said, "Gretch, thick." He touched his lips with his fingers.

She opened the door, her hand on her heart and her voice choked up, so Telly finished, "…and thin." Telly entered, reaching out to wrap her in his embrace. Sophie jumped on his leg eagerly, and he bent over to pat her head. "Daddy missed you too," he told her.

Gretchen melted into him. He felt her shudder, and he rubbed her back. "I'm sorry I did what I did, but I got lost in the moment." He kissed her on the lips. "I missed you."

"I missed you too."

"Then why'd you leave?"

"I got so mad, I don't know what happened." Gretchen said in a rush. "I was so angry."

"You never get mad."

Gretchen looked up at him, her blue eyes wide. "I know. I don't know what came over me, but I got stuck in the anger. You know I don't care about money, Telly."

He laughed in agreement. "What happened at work?" Telly sat down on the pullout couch in the tiny room. "Something had to occur to make you so upset." The room was so small that if Telly stretched his arms sideways, he could touch the Billy Joel and Bon Jovi posters on the facing walls. "You were comfortable here?" He looked at the pile of men's socks and underwear shoved under a lamp table.

Gretchen nodded. "I felt safe. Your parents are so nice. I didn't want to stay in the house."

Telly nodded. His parents must be going deaf, because their conversations were so loud they could be heard two doors down. "Manny's a slob." Telly looked at the stack of pizza boxes on the small counter that separated a tiny utility kitchen.

"He's a boy and never grew up. They indulge him."

"What happened at work?" Telly put his feet up and made himself comfortable on the couch. He pulled Gretchen into the curve of his arm, caressed her shoulder.

She shrugged, her face downcast. "Rob wants me to come to one of his parties this week. He said if I don't come, I won't have a job. I don't want to go."

"You should have told me." He kissed her blond head. "I don't want you doing that. The poker thing, it's not important. In the end, it wasn't even fun anymore."

"I don't think driving a cab is going to be a barrel of laughs either. You took the job at George's?"

"I start tonight. It's not my chosen career, but it will do for now. I don't want you going back to Rob Couts or the bar."

"We need my job."

"No, we don't."

"What if it doesn't work out? We have to have a backup. I'll give two weeks' notice and finish up with them."

"He'll expect you to come to his party."

"No, he won't. Especially after I give notice. It won't matter."

The taxi thing was too new; they couldn't risk putting all their eggs in one basket, Gretchen argued, so Telly negotiated it down to a week's notice. "You should have been a lawyer," Gretchen said and kissed him. He grabbed her bag, and they headed back to their apartment.

Harriet and Frank watched them leave from the front picture window.

"You worried?" Frank asked, a frown on his face.

"I'm always worried. A master's degree in computer science, and he wants to be a poker player? I never heard of such a thing."

"I always wanted to be a pianist." Frank shrugged. He was eating an apple.

"Don't make a mess," she commanded. Harriet lifted one shoulder dismissively, letting the vertical blind fall back into place. "You couldn't. We had three little kids. You always worked."

"What about Manny? You don't complain about his acting."

Harriet clicked her tongue. "What else can he do? After his breakdown, he couldn't do much of anything else. We're lucky he's getting out of bed in the morning. Gidget's got the kids and barely makes enough to survive—ugh, forget about that husband of hers." She shuddered. "Telly doesn't have the luxury of following his dreams. He will have to take care of Manny when we're gone. Besides, he has Gretchen, and it's time he settled down."

"A few years ago you said she wasn't good enough. You thought she was after his money."

"A few years ago, he had money. He's almost thirty-four. She's devoted to him. I like her now." She went into the kitchen to get him a napkin. "Things are different. We had expectations for each of them."

Frank followed her and pulled up a stool to the immaculate counter. "You have to stop managing their lives."

"Who's managing their lives?" she asked, her voice shrill. "Who could even try? Giddy married that man, and we were lucky they decided to live in Florida instead of return to his home in Morocco. We sent Telly to the best schools. The best schools," she repeated, jabbing her finger for effect. She started to pull out lunch items. "You want a grilled cheese sandwich?"

Frank shook his head, throwing the apple core into the trash. "I'm not hungry yet. It's early." She ignored him as she set up two slices of bread and started cutting cheese.

"And Manny?" Frank persisted, coming up behind her.

"What are you talking about?" she asked impatiently. The aroma of whole wheat toast frying in butter permeated the room.

"We were talking about the kids. Manny, you set different expectations for them. Make me one of those too, please."

Harriet started on the second sandwich. "Who knew? I thought bipolar was a retirement duplex in Alaska. Who knew?" she repeated, disappointment souring her face. "I had such plans for them."

"You have different standards for the kids."

"Telly may be the middle child, but he's always been the most reliable of the three of them—at least until this poker business. Telly always did his homework, cleaned his room. He's dependable, so the job is going to have to fall on him. He doesn't have a choice." She placed the golden sandwiches on a plate and leaned over to watch him eat.

"That's not especially fair." His mouth was full.

"Who says life is fair? Was it fair for you? Or me?" Harriet demanded. "You think I didn't want to do whatever I felt like? There were bills to pay, dinners, shopping, homework, drum lessons, soccer practice. Life is about choices—could I get a manicure or have a cleaning woman? Or braces for Telly? Dance for Giddy? You think I didn't know how you hated doing the lawn or painting the house? It's what we did. It's what *he* has to do. Don't get me started on your parents, Frank—your sister did nothing for them. The whole thing fell on us when your mom broke her hip."

"That's the point. He's not married, and he doesn't have kids; if he wants to spread his wings, now's the time."

Harriet shook her head. "You put the crazy ideas in his head, Frank. He's supposed to work, and that's it. He was the smart one, the responsible child. We spent more on his education than the others'. The only wings he should spread are on the turkey he's going to make for Thanksgiving when he invites the family over. It's what you did. It's his legacy."

"He can't have us in that shithole he's staying in."

"He won't be there for long. He made big money, and he'll do it again. He is going to get a job. He's not trying hard enough. Oh, I know he says there's nothing around.

He's doing the same thing when he didn't want to take calculus."

Frank laughed. "The summer of mono."

Harriet smirked. "He had us all fooled. But in the end, he took calculus, got an A, and ended up taking the advanced course."

"But a taxi, Harriet?" Frank looked at her.

"I know Telly. He will drive the cab, and within a week a job will turn up. Maybe he'll meet someone in the car, and they'll see his potential and give him a job."

"Like a corporate fairy godmother?"

"Oh, Frank." She hit his arm. "You'll see," she said with a nod. "Something will turn up. It always does."

Frank shook his head and sighed. No matter how old the kids were, it seemed he still had to worry about them. All of them. "What's for dinner?" he asked as they wandered into the living room to watch the traffic on the street.

CHAPTER SIXTEEN

Clutch followed a group into the Culinary School of Nevada. He cruised the hallways, floating in the crowd, going into the different classrooms. He stood for a good twenty minutes watching a French chef slice up a radish so that it resembled a flower. There was a room for pastry, one with breads, and an auditorium where they were discussing the nutritional value of meals. The school was a hive of knowledge, and the one thing Clutch was sure of was he wanted his daughter to attend. It would be good for her. He sauntered into the administrative offices, sliding a folder with admissions information under his jacket. It disappeared with him out the door. *Why didn't I know about this before? It's not like there are instructions like my poker books, are there?* he wondered. Not that it was all his fault. *It was Jenny's fault too,* he huffed. He didn't see her making any plans for their kid.

Clutch felt himself pulled downtown toward the courts. He hated courts. The last time he'd entered a courtroom, he had ended up serving time for almost six years. He closed his eyes and thought about that day almost forty-eight years ago. Some things get lost to time, and some things are so razor sharp they continue to cut you with their wicked edges. He could see that courtroom in his head just like it was yesterday.

Buster sat in the front row, squeezed into a white plantation suit, his sweat-stained Stetson hanging on his fat knee. Buster's red face was drenched with perspiration, and he wiped it with a rusty, wrinkled handkerchief. Every so often, Clutch glanced at his grandfather's angry face. Alf, his cousin, sat next to the old man, shaking his head.

It was a sure thing—all he'd had to do was drive. They were hitting a fur storage; he wasn't actually stealing anything. Nobody knew North Las Vegas like Clutch Henderson. It was really a favor, he'd told Buster. "I owed the guy."

"You stupid ass," Buster replied. "I wasted all that time teaching you the game, but you never learned nuthin'."

"I'm the best player this side of the Strip," Clutch boasted. "I could outplay you anytime. When this is over, I'll show you."

"You ain't nothing but a punk. You don't know how to play poker…never could. I pumped you up to make you feel good, but you are just a two-bit hustler."

"I'm good." Clutch told him, his voice full of hatred.

"If you were good, why'd you get involved with them?" Buster pointed to the other defendants.

"I owed too much."

"You owed too much 'cause you played like shit, you cocky motherfucker. You think you know everything. I wouldn't waste another minute on you. You ruined your grandmother's life," Buster told him. "You and me, we're finished. You'll never be anything, Oliver, cause you break everything that falls into your clutches."

Alf laughed, "So that's why you call him Clutch, Gramps?"

"I call him Clutch because he squeezes everything worthwhile in life until there ain't nothing left but dust." Buster's gold bracelet winked in the sunlight that streamed in through the tall windows. "You like my Series bracelet, loser? Well, enjoy it from there, because that's the closest you'll ever come to it."

"I'll win one on my own when I get out," Clutch called after him, stung by his grandfather's fury. "You called me Clutch 'cause I knew how to clutch the cards right!" he shot back with venom.

Buster turned, his voice equally loud. "You'll never win a gold bracelet—you don't have the skill, and I'll never teach you another move."

"I can outplay you anytime, Grandpa. Name it and I'll kick your—"

Buster spun, his face gleaming with sweat under the harsh lights. "The next time we play poker it will be in hell, when the devil comes to take his due."

His grandfather turned his back, leaving Clutch to be cuffed and led away. He never saw him again.

Buster was furious, but he'd paid for a good lawyer. Clutch served half the sentence and got out with good behavior.

Both Ruth and Buster died while he was serving time, and the bracelet, along with the rest of Buster's estate, went to his cousin, Alf.

"I loved that bracelet," he mused. "It was supposed to be mine. Not to mention the old house and its contents." With his mind on the past, he didn't notice that the courtroom was beginning to fill, with Ginny and some fancy suit on one side and Ruby and Jenny on the other.

"All rise..." Clutch automatically stood as the judge entered the courtroom. She was attractive, he thought, her red hair pulled off her head in a bun, half-moon glasses hanging from a chain that rested on her black robe.

The proceedings began with Jenny's lawyer. He was just a kid. He noticed Ruby had changed into a black dress; the face jewelry was gone, and her hair was neatly combed. The boy wonder stood in his ill-fitting suit and argued that the case was cut and dried—Oliver and Jennifer were legally married according to state laws. They were there to determine the rights of the parties in respect to the division of Oliver Henderson's estate. As there was no will, the laws of succession applied, he told the court reasonably. Jenny sat, her legs crossed, all wounded dignity. She was the mother of Oliver's only child; at the very least, the lawyer said, the money should be held in trust until Ruby came into her majority.

"That's all very touching," the other lawyer began, "but Oliver and Jennifer were married on paper only. It was a well-known fact that they both desired to be divorced. Gineva Garcia was Clutch Henderson's common-law wife. They had lived continuously together for over ten years. Clearly, Jennifer lost all her rights based on their separation."

"Just because Gineva Garcia was his girlfriend doesn't entitle her to anything," Jenny's lawyer stated. "You can't be a common-law wife to someone who is still married. That's bigamy."

"Jennifer Henderson had Mr. Henderson arrested and took out a restraining order against him. Is that the action of a loving wife?"

"Loving or not, Your Honor, the fact is she was indeed still his wife."

"So was Ginny Garcia."

"Objection. As previously stated, you can't be a common-law wife to someone who is married."

"Sustained," the judge said in a mildly bored voice.

Clutch looked at all the players. Jenny had always been a good actress. Occasionally, she took out a crumpled tissue to sob prettily into its depths.

His daughter and the boy lawyer kept exchanging long, hot looks at each other. He walked behind him, bent down, and whispered, "She's jailbait, pal. Not even seventeen yet." Wait, maybe she was seventeen...what year was she born, exactly? Clutch couldn't seem to remember. "Don't matter, son. Underage is underage."

Ruby appeared human today. Twice, he reached forward, ready to smack the lawyer in the back of his head when he ogled her legs. Man, but that skirt was short. *What is her mother thinking?* he wondered. He walked over to her and tugged her collar over her slight cleavage.

Ruby sat up, startled, when she felt her shirt pulled together over her chest.

Ginny was skittish; she kept looking at a man in the rear of the room. He looked familiar, but Clutch couldn't place him. Most of the time, Ginny kept her head lowered. He caught her giving Ruby a sweet, apologetic smile, which was heartily returned. Clutch saw Ginny sigh deeply and then look at the man in the back again. Her furrowed brows told him she was nervous. He wandered over, taking a seat next to the man, studying his profile. Who was this guy, and why was he watching Ginny?

Court was adjourned. Ginny hurried out, the man following her out the courtroom doors.

Clutch sauntered after them, speeding up to move in front of them. The man caught Ginny by the arm. "I'll take you home," he said.

"No." She pulled her arm away. "Don't you see where things are going? They are never going to award that money to me. You have to stop."

"The kid might get it."

"Yes, and she's underage, so it won't be available for a couple of years. Who knows what will be left once his wife gets hold of it. She'll be the trustee. Give it up, Victor."

"Victor Mazzone!" Clutch grumbled. His loan shark. He owed him big, over a million with interest. *Man, that shit compounds daily,* he thought. *Might be close to two already.*

"Look, I did it. I took her to court. I contested the will. I told you, I am nothing in Clutch's estate. They aren't going to give me anything. You wasted your money on that lawyer," Ginny said with a plaintive voice.

"Hardly nothing, Gin—I loved you," Clutch said without thinking. Ginny didn't register. Why couldn't she hear him? Telly did. Clutch swallowed and said it again, louder.

Ginny looked around. "Did…did you hear that?"

"Hear what? It's not over. I have to get paid," Victor said.

She shrugged indifferently. "You can't take blood from a stone. You made a bad investment in Clutch."

"You talking from experience?" Victor said sarcastically.

Ginny gave him a hard look, but Clutch knew by her expression that she was conflicted. He'd give anything to get inside her head right now.

Victor went on, "What do you got to show for sticking by that loser for ten years?"

Clutch considered Victor, knowing he never once told her he loved her while he was alive.

"What exactly did you see in that guy?" Victor asked.

Ginny opened her mouth to reply. "He was so…so…" She was struggling to find words. Her mouth snapped shut. It appeared that Ginny couldn't quite remember what was so special about Clutch after all. "I don't want to talk to you anymore, Mr. Mazzone. I think our business is done."

Victor continued as if she hadn't spoken. "If the kid gets the money, you're right. I won't see it for a couple of years. So…" He lowered his voice while he grabbed her arm. Clutch moved forward, ready to plow into him. "You'll sign over your house to me."

"That's mine."

"Yeah, and as Clutch's common law wife, you're going to give it to me."

"Didn't you hear them in there? I am not his wife. I'm nothing to him. He left me nothing. I'll be homeless."

Victor shrugged. "Look, lady, I have to get mine. That's the nature of this business. Like, I'm real sorry, but I have a business to run."

Ginny staggered away, Clutch following to make sure she got home safely. He sat on the couch for a long time watching her do a crossword puzzle. The plants were dying, and she didn't care. He had placed a watering can where she would notice it, but she kept walking past it without registering it was there. Clutch put his feet up and his hands behind his head, and for a moment, it brought him back in time to last year, Ginny's domestic sounds filling their home. He almost felt like calling out for her to make him something to eat. He pulled out the application for cooking school but gave up trying to read it. It slid in between the cushions of the couch.

The afternoon waned, and Clutch rose. He walked over to Ginny, who worked dispiritedly at the counter preparing her dinner. He wrapped his arms around her, feeling her shiver. Placing his ghostly lips on her neck, he kissed her gently, standing there enjoying the feel of her. She brushed her neck impatiently, irritated. Eventually, he left, leaving Ginny to stare out the window and wonder if she was grieving for Clutch or for herself.

CHAPTER SEVENTEEN

Telly kissed Gretchen on the cheek. "Don't wait up for me," he told her. "You sure you didn't lock up that money?" They had come home and searched thoroughly. The money was gone.

"Positive. It was on the coffee table when I left. I don't want it, Telly. It was dirty money."

"You believe me about Clutch then?" he asked her, his face earnest.

Gretchen tilted her blond head. "I find the whole thing hard to believe, Telly; maybe it was all a dream. Either way, it's over, all right? You'll never mention Clutch or poker again." She was feeling better already. Gretchen sat on the bed, her legs curled under her, her hand protectively over her belly. She wanted to tell him, but not just yet. He was still so unsettled.

"Looks like he's gone." Telly bounced around the room, looking under the dusty orange drapes.

"Let's just forget about Clutch," Gretchen said with relief. "New beginnings." She smiled sweetly at him. Telly walked over to kiss her tenderly and then left. She decided she would share her news with him tonight.

From the doorway he called, "Thick..."

She responded with a satisfied, "Thin." Her hand rested over her heart.

Telly made it down to the garage and was given a 2014 yellow cab. Bob the mechanic went over the air conditioning and gave him a brief summary on the paperwork. It was sixty-forty—he got the larger number and could work for the next twelve hours. Some guys pulled in three to four hundred a night. Best news was they told him he would get paid every day, in cash. Gretchen could quit; he couldn't wait to tell her.

Telly pulled out as the city lights started to blink on, the purple dusk bathing the evening sky. It was quiet, the squawk of the speaker the only disruption. His first call was to Harrah's. He pulled into the cab line. A purple and beige uniformed doorman waved him in while his whistle shrieked. It was a trip to the airport. He got out to shove ten suitcases into the trunk. He couldn't close it. He piled four of the bags in the front seat.

"Don't you have a bungee?" the doorman asked.

"Uh...no."

"Here," he said, handing Telly a neon and red bungee cord. "Stuff the luggage in, and then tie the trunk with this."

Telly pulled out a five-dollar bill, tipping the doorman. Clutch's expression, "Give big, get big," was ringing in his ears.

The passengers had lost, but they'd had a ball. Brenda and Warren were heading back to New Jersey. "Could we stop at In-N-Out just one more time?" Brenda pleaded.

"What time's your flight?"

"We have three hours."

Telly made the turn by Excalibur, pulling in through the window. The couple called out their order, laughing so hard they had tears of joy. "One for the road!" Brenda shouted. Warren laughed uproariously.

"I got it." Telly smiled, paying the fourteen dollars for their dinner. *Give big, get big*—the words echoed in the car.

"Give big, get big, *you dope*. You're not going to get anything from these rubes." Clutch's voice reverberated through the car.

Telly gasped. Clutch was back, sitting on Brenda's lap. "I'll say this for her: she's got a nice rack," he said.

Telly looked in the rearview mirror, his eyes wide. Brenda must have noticed his expression because she said, "Don't worry. We'll pay you back when we get to the airport and I can get to my purse."

"No, no, it's fine." He raced down Industrial toward the airport.

"What's the rush?" Warren demanded as they swerved down the road. "Take it easy."

"I don't want you to miss your flight," he told them.

Minutes later, he pulled up to the terminal. They got out, and Telly hauled their luggage, making a stack on the sidewalk.

"Well, that was interesting," Warren said as he took out a hundred dollars.

Telly pulled out money to make change.

"No, keep the change," Warren said with a laugh. "You deserve it. You were as generous as you were entertaining."

Telly thanked him and then jumped back into the cab.

"What are you doing here?" he hissed at Clutch.

"We have to make the entry fee."

"No, we don't. I am not doing that anymore. I think you cured me from playing poker ever again. I don't even like it anymore."

They passed rows of strip clubs. Clutch made appreciative noises when they sped past the tall marquees with barely dressed women advertising each club. "Well, that's not encouraging. Hey, let's stop here. They have great—what? I was going to say tacos! They make tacos."

"I don't care. Now get out of my cab and out of my life."

"No can do, Telly. We have to make the entry fee tonight. Dump this banana and let's play poker."

"Not going to happen."

"Well, then, it looks like I'm riding shotgun until you change your mind." Clutch settled comfortably into the backseat.

Telly pulled violently to the side of the road. The hot Vegas heat hit him like a blast furnace when he exited the car. He opened the rear door. "Get out!" he shouted.

A homeless man wheeling a shiny metal supermarket cart was walking on the dirt-packed side of the road. He wore filthy clothes and a greasy fishing hat, with iron-gray hair escaping on either side like Bozo the Clown. He stopped, scratching his back. Leaning down, he peered into the dark interior of the car.

He looked up at Telly, then down again. Telly was screaming that if Clutch didn't get out, he was going to drag him out. Clutch sat in the car laughing hysterically. Telly leaned down, trying to grab him, only to have his hands come up empty.

The old geezer in the street came closer, looking to see who Telly was fighting with. His rheumy eyes searched the backseat.

"Who you talking to?" he asked. "Wanna drink?" He pulled out a whiskey bottle from a brown paper bag in the front of the cart.

Telly was breathing hard, frustrated, just about at his wit's end. He kicked a rock by his foot. The rock barely moved; the earth was hard packed and dry as a bone.

"You're stuck with me until I decide to move on, so get used to it," Clutch said between his chuckles. "You need this win as much as I do. You'll never have a shred of confidence if you don't see this through."

"I don't need you to build my confidence," Telly responded.

"You don't have a choice here, partner. You lost your choice when you made that wish simultaneously with me."

"Be reasonable," Telly pleaded and then realized that the bum was peering into the car, offering him a drink. "A bee," he told him as he waved his arms. "A bee flew into the car."

"Killer bee?"

"I don't know." Telly was exasperated.

"Beware those killer bees; they'll get ya." He made a snatching movement with his filthy, long-nailed fingers. Telly swallowed hard. The old man snapped loudly. "Wham, you're a dead man."

Telly gulped again, his voice a whisper. "It wasn't a killer bee."

"Good." The bum saluted him and then shuffled off, wheeling his possessions down the road.

"You be reasonable," Clutch's voice pulled him back. "We've got twelve hours to make it to the entry. I know you can borrow from the Quick Daddy guy. Let's go."

Telly ignored him. "I'm working. I'll wait until you get bored enough to leave me alone and find another sucker." He slammed the door, jumped in, and put the car in drive to head for his next pickup.

He had a pickup at Luxor, a drop at the Nugget. Two trips to McCarran Airport. All in all, it wasn't as bad as he'd thought it was going to be. People were having fun. Winning or losing didn't seem to matter. He made small talk and was pleasantly surprised when they tipped him. He called Gretchen but turned away so Clutch couldn't hear what he said.

* * *

Gretchen rubbed the sleep from her eyes and picked up the phone. "You OK, Tel?" He sounded nervous.

"Fine," Telly insisted loudly, then repeated more softly, "Fine; it's not bad. I actually like it."

"Good, good," Gretchen yawned. "I'm so proud of you. Love you."

"Love you too," Telly said sincerely. He slid his phone back into his pocket, got into the car, and gave the ghost the silent treatment. Clutch hung from the ceiling of the car, dangled his feet out the rear, and felt up the female passengers. Telly steadfastly refused to look at him.

He ignored Clutch when he stretched across the passengers' laps and looked in the other direction when he opened their purses or stuck his fingers in Telly's ears. Telly slammed the door in the ghost's face when he left to grab a bite at an Ethiopian restaurant the cabbies all talked about. The food was great; he wasn't sure what he had, but the rice was incredible. He stalled before getting back into the car, staying longer with Gretchen on the phone for his second call than he was supposed to. Clutch tried to distract him, but Telly tuned him out, refusing to acknowledge him no matter how outrageously he behaved. By four in the morning, Telly had made a few hundred dollars. He was nearing his shift's end when he pulled into the Wynn. The line was always long there, but someone had told him it was a good door for tips. The doorman whistled for his attention, and Telly slid into place. The door opened, and a man fell into the backseat, clearly drunk. "Take me downtown! No, never mind. Take me to the desert, and leave me there to die!" he slurred. He sighed so deeply it reverberated through the car.

"Bad night?" Telly asked sympathetically.

"Bad week—no, bad year…"

"Bad life…" Clutch finished. "This oughta be fun. Roy Rogers been drinking?" Clutch was mildly bored.

Momentarily diverted, Telly asked, "Who?"

"Not who, where. I changed my mind. Take me downtown. Binions," the older man demanded.

"Roy Rogers? You don't know Roy Rogers? He was a famous singing cowboy from the fifties," Clutch informed him.

"Before my time," Telly said, shaking his head.

"Look, kid, I know Binions is an old place, but I like the atmosphere. These new casinos are like hospitals—antiseptic, you know. They don't have any mojo." He sighed gustily. "I don't feel comfortable here anymore. I wish I'd never come."

Telly realized he'd answered Clutch instead of his patron. He looked at the passenger in the rearview mirror. He wore a white Stetson and a cowboy shirt. He was definitely on the later side of sixty. The man tipped up his hat so he could make eye contact with Telly.

Telly shrugged. "They all seem alike to me."

"Are you kidding me? Casinos used to be fun. Now it's all computer games, sweet-smelling perfume, and loud music. I like to smell sweat."

"I miss the good old days," Clutch said wistfully.

The passenger complained: "We used to come here all the time, m'wife and me. Had a ball. They treated us like a king and queen. Anything we wanted—show tickets, dinner with Sinatra, boat rides on Lake Mead, you name it. It's like I don't fit in anymore here. Kids everywhere, messing up the rhythm of the tables. I feel like I've lived my time, like I'm almost invisible. They—"

"They?" Telly asked, looking at him in the rearview mirror.

"You know, the younger generation. They make me feel useless. Like I don't have anything relevant to add. I miss my wife. I miss my old life." He ended the sentence, his voice barely audible.

"I'm sure you have plenty to contribute to whatever you do. You have experience. You can't buy that. You look like you have a lot to offer."

"Looks can be deceiving. I loved my wife. I liked being married. She died four years ago, and I really struggled. Then this year, I met a gal. She's really nice, but she's still stuck on her guy as well."

"Break up?"

Stan shook his head. "He died last year. Well, she told me she wasn't ready yet. Do you know how hard it was for me to approach her? I didn't want to even come here again; I miss being with my wife. She always knew what to do. I figured if I could just get a sign from her…a message…but that psychic would only meet me here on her western tour. It was the only reading she had for me."

"What psychic?" Telly asked.

"Georgia Oaken, the TV medium from Long Island. She was performing here. I had my office call, but that was it. Here and on Tuesday. Everything went to shit when m'wife passed away. Cancer, you know." Telly nodded sympathetically. "Been working at the grindstone for over fifty years. I built my business with my bare hands." He held up his hands as if Telly could envision their capabilities. "It's this new generation. The kids don't respect me. The minute I open my mouth, I see them roll their eyes. They think they know everything. It's ruining everything for me. I don't think I can do anything anymore. Especially not alone."

"Tell me about it," Clutch chimed in.

Telly nodded. "I know how you feel. But seems to me you have a few choices…mister…"

"Stan. Stan Jarvis. What's your name?"

"Telly."

"Tell me, Telly, what choices do you see?"

"It's simple. You have to reinvent yourself."

"What are you talking about?" Both Clutch and Stan said it at the same time. Telly smiled.

"Sometimes when you don't fit in, no matter how old you are, no matter how set in your ways, you have to make a new mold."

Stan leaned forward, sticking his head through the opening. "Oh, I don't know," he said with a dismissive wave of his hand. "Sounds like too much work."

"No such thing. Nature changes, rivers and mountains change. What makes us think we have to stay the same? If everybody is telling you that you can't dance, you can either sit down or learn a new dance."

Stan digested Telly's statement for a few minutes. He opened his mouth and closed it again. "It's so simple," he said to himself. "You're a bright guy. Think it'll work on the ladies?"

Telly shrugged. "Don't see why it wouldn't. Maybe if she sees you in a new light, she'll be more interested." Telly watched the emotions play over Stan's face. "Her guy died, right? Your wife died too. Maybe your grief reminds her too much of her own. So, try a different tactic."

"Huh." Stan sat back in the seat, deep in thought. "Never thought about it that way before. Have you ever reinvented yourself?" Stan sat up eagerly.

"I'm working on it. If you are being minimized, then it's up to you to maximize yourself and make them take notice."

"You play craps?"

"I like poker," Telly told him and then added hastily, "but I don't play anymore." He ignored Clutch's loud snort.

"Too slow for me. Hey, come on in with me, and we'll play a game or two."

Telly shook his head. "Sorry, I—"

"I'll pay for your time." Stan insisted.

"I just can't," Telly said. "I'm on duty."

"I'm on duty! What are you, a cop?" Clutch climbed over the front seat through the protective shield. "Are you nuts? This guy's a high roller. This is our chance, Telly."

"I also promised someone I wouldn't play poker," Telly retored to both Clutch and Stan.

"Look, I'm calling your boss. If he says it's OK, you're coming in with me. I like you. You make sense, Tony."

"Telly," he corrected him.

"Like Kojak?"

"Yes, but I can't..."

The passenger took off his hat, revealing his hairless pate. "We're bald brothers, you know—like blood, only sexier. This is amazing. Now, you have to come in with me. It's a sign from my Irma that things are going to change."

"I don't have any money!" Telly's face broke out into a sweat. "And I'm not bald." He turned furiously to Clutch, whispering, "Are you doing this? Because if you are, it's not working."

"Hello, this is Stan Jarvis. I'm in one of your cabs, and I want the driver, Telly, to go into Binions with me while I play a game of craps. What's your last name, Tel?"

"Martin…but I can't go in. I'll lose my—"

Stan wasn't listening. "Look, I'm putting five C-notes in an envelope for Telly to bring to you if you let him go in with me. Yeah…yeah, OK, a grand. Yes…hold on." He handed the phone to Telly. "I put it on speaker; he wants to talk to you."

"Telly, you do whatever Mr. Jarvis tells you to," the dispatcher was adamant.

"But my shift is almost over."

"Don't matter—just bring the car and my grand back when you finish. Stay with Mr. Jarvis," his boss said.

"Binions! I am in heaven." Clutch was ecstatic. "Do you know, Telly, that's where the poker tournaments started." He ruffled Telly's hair. "I hope the dice are hot. Never mind that," Clutch said, watching a pair of women in short, sequined dresses enter the building. "I know the women are hot! Woo hoo!"

"Stay close to me, Telly," Stan told him as they walked through the smoke-filled casino.

A smarmy man in an ill-fitting suit approached them with his hand outstretched. "Stanley! I was afraid you left us for the fancy bright lights of the Strip."

"Left you?" Stan laughed. "How could I leave you when the good steaks and bad women are all here?"

Telly's eyes stung from the pall of smoke. The subtle chink of chips was muted in the thick air. The place was filled with an older crowd. Looking around, he realized that nobody but him had their real hair color. The wait-staff was ancient but spry, as they walked the floor with trays filled with drinks. There were no umbrellas in any of the drinks here.

"This way—stay close to me." Stan stepped lively toward the center of the casino.

"Who's that with you, Stanley?"

"This is Telly. I was feeling a bit poorly, and he snapped me right out of it. Do you know what that calls for?"

"What, Stan?" the host asked.

"A crap game always makes me feel better!" He slapped him on the back. Telly hung behind them. "Belly up to the table, son. Get me a marker, Clay," he called out to the pit boss.

"How much, sir?"

"Start with a hundred, and then we'll see how it goes."

"He's getting a marker for a hundred dollars? That's crazy," Telly muttered.

"It's a hundred thousand, Tel. You landed us in a great pile of manure. This guy's filthy with it!" Clutch told him, his eyes alight with excitement.

The whole rack was filled with chips. Stan placed a stack of black on the tray in front of Telly. Telly looked at him, his eyebrows raised.

"You can't shoot if you're not on the pass line," Stan explained.

"I can't shoot at all," Telly told him.

"Everybody can shoot." The dealer moved a row of six sets of bright red dice toward them.

"Pick the pair that speaks to you," Stan told him. "Make sure you hit the back wall, and don't overthink it. Oh, and put a hundred on the hard eight," Stan advised him. "We're about to reinvent you."

"I really can't." Telly was miserable.

"Yes, you can. You can do anything," Stan told him. "You are doing this for me, and I appreciate it. You pulled me out of a place so dark, Telly. You have to finish what we started." He pulled him close. "I was going to blow my brains out tonight. You gave me purpose. You made me want to—"

"Bet the hard eight, Telly!" Clutch spoke in a rush, interrupting them, lost to everything but the game. "I never bet the sucker bets, but this might be our lucky day."

Telly put one hundred on the pass line, his hand shaking. He'd saved Stan's life; he felt responsible for him. Just one game, for Stan. He felt like his old self, comfortable with doing for others. Stan put five black chips on his. He picked up another hundred, looking at the squares in the center showing the hard ways. "Do it, Telly!" Clutch yelled.

Telly threw the black chip toward the middle. "One hundred on the hard eight."

"Pair of squares. I love it." Stan threw two black chips and one green one next to Telly's. "Two hundred for me, twenty-five for the boys," he said, placing a bet for the dealers at the table, who all smiled with approval. "Now go get us that hard eight, Telly."

Telly chose the center dice and rubbed them together in his sweaty hands.

"One hand!" the pit boss yelled. "Only one hand."

"Shake the bones, then let 'em fly!" Clutch yelled in his other ear.

Telly dropped his other hand, shook his right hand, then threw the dice to the other end of the table. Everybody craned their necks. Stan and Clutch whooped and then Clutch screamed, "Ozzie and Harriet! Pair of squares!" Stan hit Telly's arm while he howled with joy.

Telly bent forward to see the dice at the other end, each one with four dots. "Oh, those are the squares," he said softly.

The dealer made three piles in the center of the table. Telly counted a stack of two hundred, eight hundred, and sixteen hundred. They pushed the largest pile to Stan, who informed them to press the eight another hundred, and put a black chip on all the other hard ways. Telly's eyes widened as they pushed the middle pile toward him.

"That's for me?"

"You bet. Press it, Telly. Put another hundred on the hard eight," Stan advised him.

The dealers thanked Stan for his bet.

"I made that." Telly was incredulous.

"Yessir. Do it again. If you get another eight, we make our point. Put five hundred dollars behind the line."

"Five hundred?" Telly questioned.

"Always bet full odds!" Clutch shouted.

Telly shrugged. It wasn't his money; he planned to give it all back to Stan anyway. He placed five black chips behind the pass line.

Stan placed chips all over the table, covering every number on the green baize. Telly gulped; there had to be six thousand dollars lying on the table.

"Just get me numbers, Telly. Lots of numbers, except the bad one."

"Do you mean the—"

"Don't! Don't say that number! Ever! Don't even think that number! We need fours, fives, sixes, eights, nines, and tens! Bring me those numbers, Telly!"

Telly shrugged and reached forward for the dice. If he tried, he couldn't remember what happened except that the smoke got denser and a crowd formed around them, growing in both size and noise, as he mechanically threw the dice, hitting the same numbers over and over again. Stan kept reaching over and throwing Telly's chips onto more squares on the table and then loading them into the tray in front of him every time he hit the number. Soon, it was a rainbow of multicolored chips. He thought Clutch was going to die all over again when they paid him with a yellow thousand-dollar chip. Truth was, Telly didn't know what was going on; it was a blur and seemed to go on forever. By the time he heard the crowd roar with disappointment, his arm ached and he was covered with sweat. Looking at his watch, he realized the entire episode had taken barely forty-five minutes, and he had made his new friend a shitload of money. It took another half hour for the pit boss to cash out Stan at two hundred and fifty thousand dollars. He paid his marker and tipped the crew.

"That was incredible," Telly told Stan, who was trying to light a congratulatory cigar. "I have to learn how to play this game."

"No, son. You just have to shoot and shoot well. Nice hand."

"Thanks, Mr. Jarvis. I have to head back and return the cab."

"Whoa, whoa, where you goin', Tel? Take your chips." Stan gestured to the loaded rack of chips.

"No, that's all yours. Thanks for a great evening."

"No, sir. Those are yours. You earned them."

"Take the money, Tel," Clutch danced around them. "We have enough to enter the Series."

"I can't." Telly started to walk away.

"Listen here, Telly. I couldn't have won without your fine shooting. So, if you want, take off my vig, the thousand I staked you with. The rest is yours. Give me your number."

"Nineteen thousand forty-five dollars," the dealer told him.

Telly opened his mouth. "I can't—"

Stan was busy talking on his phone. He sounded playful, and he distinctly heard him flirting. Maybe he was trying that new strategy with his lady friend. He sounded happy enough.

Telly shrugged and told the dealer to take off five hundred for the dealers.

"Nicely done, Telly—give big, get big," Clutch said.

Stan turned. "Tel, don't leave without giving me your number."

Telly dutifully wrote his phone number on a card. "Thank you."

"No, thank you. Good luck in the Series."

"Oh, I can't—" he started to say, but Stan turned to talk to his host.

Clutch poked him in the shoulder. "Ow, that hurt." Telly started walking toward the cashier. "I don't know how I'm going to explain this to Gretchen."

"You were working, baby." Clutch walked alongside him.

He entered the valet, gave his ticket, and waited for his cab. Clutch slid into the front seat next to him.

"Where do you think you're going?" Telly asked him as he shifted into drive.

"Head to Mandalay."

"Mandalay? I'm bringing the car back and heading home. Gretchen should be waking up soon."

Clutch reached out to grab the steering wheel. The car swerved to the right. "Stop that!"

"Registration is today. You have the money. We're in."

"In your dreams. I told you, I'm not playing poker. I have to return the car."

"No way!" Clutch sneered. "You made a promise to me."

"I made a more important one to Gretchen. Count me out."

The car started to fill with a gray fog. Telly waved his hands, having difficulty seeing. He opened the side window, sticking his head out to try to navigate the road.

"You ain't seen nothing yet. As my old grandpappy used to say, 'When you got 'em by the nuts, squeeze!' I'm gonna squeeze yours until you sing soprano."

"I don't care. I made a promise to Gretchen that I won't break." Telly felt the car accelerate until he was going ninety in a fifty-mile-per-hour zone. Sirens screamed behind him, but Clutch wouldn't let go of the gas pedal. "You're going to get me arrested," Telly said through gritted teeth.

"So?" Clutch struggled with the wheel. It was as though they were in a tug-of-war. Cars were honking; he was a menace on the road. The siren was louder, closer, right behind him. Telly pulled over, slammed the car in park, and took the keys out of the ignition. He opened the door to fall out on the hard-packed dirt.

"What do you think you were doing back there?" the highway patrolman demanded.

"The gas pedal got stuck. I tried to stop." Telly held up his hands.

"License and registration," the cop said.

"By the time I get through with you, your license will be suspended," Clutch threatened. "Nobody will hire you."

"I could—"

"You could what, Mr. Martin?" the officer asked without looking up. "You've been drinking?"

"No, sir." Telly felt Clutch's hot breath on his neck.

"Still, maybe you should come in with me." The patrolman observed him steadily.

"Aw, come on. I'm fine. It was the cab. Gas pedal was stuck."

The cop lifted his sunglasses to look at Telly and handed him three tickets while issuing a stern warning.

"That's all going on your record. By tomorrow, you'll be fired from the cab service. Remember they have a no-tolerance policy," Clutch taunted.

"I'll tell them it was the gas pedal. The cop believed it."

"Go ahead. I can't wait to see Bob the mechanic throw you out of there."

Telly walked back to the cab, knowing it was true. Looking at the three citations, he knew the job was finished. He was going to have to find something else. At least he had the winnings to live on for now.

"Oh no you don't," Clutch told him as he slid into the car. "You have to use at least ten Gs to buy into the Series."

"I told you, I'm finished with poker."

"Telly," Clutch said earnestly. "The way I see it, you don't have much of a choice. I'm gonna haunt your ass for the rest of your miserable life. Mine will be the first face you see when you open your eyes and the last when you go to sleep at night. I'm not leaving without that bracelet, and you're the only person who can get it for me. Let me tell you something, partner. You're gonna see my face when you turn on the television. I will be in the air you breathe. Admittedly, I've been pretty tame."

Telly snorted.

"Oh, I've been behaving, believe me. I can get real nasty. In fact, I think I can get real nasty around Gretchen. I plan to make a believer—"

Telly slammed his foot on the brake, reaching over to swing at Clutch. His fist went through cold air.

"Telly, Telly, Telly. You can't hurt me—I'm dead. But I can hurt you." Clutch was now in the backseat. Telly felt his head being grabbed. "Let's play a little game I've learned." The car moved into drive; the steering wheel jerked to life; and the car headed toward an overpass. "This would be so easy for me, Telly. I can smash this car against the concrete, and then we'll be together for eternity." The car accelerated, heading for the concrete barricade. Clutch hummed a song. Telly punched the brake with his foot, but the car kept moving. Grabbing the wheel, he spun it, but the course never changed. "End it, Telly, or I'll end it. Tell me you'll play or die, Telly. The choice is yours."

Telly felt the car jump the curb, the wall coming up fast. *Where's the highway patrol when you need them?* he thought. "All right!" he screamed. "I'll play." The car stopped so suddenly, Telly's neck snapped. His heart pounded like an oil pump in his chest. He was breathing so hard, he could barely talk. He reached into his pocket, found his asthma inhaler, and took a dose. He turned around to see Clutch sitting smugly in the back of the cab. "I always liked playing chicken when I was a kid."

"If I do this, you will be out of my life?"

"Forever," Clutch said sincerely. "And ever."

Telly returned the cab and took the bus to the Mandalay Convention Center without calling Gretchen. He walked through the crowds, his head down, his face devoid of expression. He was so angry his jaw hurt. *How am I going to explain this to Gretchen?* he thought. He'd register and then go home and break it to her. Hordes of poker buffs milled around waiting to get in lines to join up for the International Series Main Event. News vans blocked the entrance of the venue behind the casino. Telly brushed past a reporter who pushed a mike in his face. The camera followed him as he got into line for registration.

"Hey, Telly!" someone shouted from behind. Stan Jarvis waved him over. He hadn't slept yet—his face looked puffy, his eyes rimmed with red.

"I thought you didn't play poker," Telly said as he walked closer to shake his hand.

"I don't, but that doesn't mean I don't place odds on winners. You signed in?"

Telly shook his head. "Not yet."

They looked at the variety of people talking in clusters. The place was packed. There was a record turnout.

"Great crowd," Stan said. He punched Telly in the shoulder playfully. "Thanks for the great advice. My girl agreed to meet me here."

Telly smiled, genuinely happy for him. "Glad it worked." He looked over his shoulder at Clutch wandering through the crowds, slapping backs and putting his arms around players he clearly knew.

"What's the matter?" Stan asked.

Telly thought about what to say and shook his head. "Nothing. Didn't sleep enough. Well, I have to go—games start at four, and I need some shut-eye before I start."

"Good luck! I'm placing my money on you."

Telly shook his head. "I don't know if I can do this," Telly said, his voice low. His eyes searched for Clutch again, and he felt a small amount of relief that he couldn't find him. It felt good to be alone.

"What? That's foolish talk. You have as good a chance as anybody. A wise man once told me that if everyone is telling you that you can't dance, try a new move. Let me tell you, Telly, you got plenty of moves. Come on, son. I'll buy you some steak and eggs," Stan told him.

Telly looked at the older man. He had repeated what Telly had told him earlier. In a weird way, it brought him a sense of peace. "Thanks, but no. I need to sleep."

"I'll be there to buy you steak and eggs after you win, then."

"You got it, Mr. Jarvis."

"Stan."

Telly quickly filled out the registration form and then headed to the cab line to get home.

CHAPTER EIGHTEEN

Chrissy stood ironing; the morning news was on. The newscaster was reporting the immense turnout for the International Series of Poker. Steam rose from her iron. It was too hot to be doing this, but Jack needed a pressed shirt at the bank. *It was a lot easier when he worked at the gym,* she thought sourly. Chrissy saw a man push past the reporter on the screen. She dropped the iron to come around and get a closer look. Squinting, she peered closely through narrowed eyes and cursed. "That's Telly Martin."

Grabbing her cell, she dialed Gretchen.

Her friend's sleepy voice answered the phone.

"I thought you said he was getting a regular job."

"Chrissy?"

"Yeah. I saw Telly."

"You saw Telly where? He's working."

"Yeah, sure he is. I just saw him on the morning news. They were covering the registration for the Series. What's going on, Gretchen? Gretchen?"

Gretchen had dropped the phone and glanced at her alarm clock. It was nine in the morning. "Telly?" she called out.

"Telly!" This time she yelled. She didn't notice that the guy in 4A didn't yell at her. He was gone too.

* * *

Ruby turned on the television to watch players register for the Series.

"Shut that shit off," Jenny called from the other room. She came in to catch a loving testimonial from Ramona Heart about Clutch.

Ruby ignored her, her eyes scanning the spots in the crowd as if she expected her father to be there somewhere. Ramona finished, and the reporter held out the mike as the camera hunted for a new person to interview. A guy with dark, shaggy hair brushed past her angrily. Clearly, he did not want to be approached. The camera followed his march to the registration lines. Ruby gasped. She got up to move closer to the screen. Pushing behind him was her father. Rubbing her eyes, she looked again, but saw only the back of the rude player, her father's image gone.

"Beloved Clutch my ass." Jenny took a congratulatory swallow of bourbon. She held up her glass for a toast. "Rot in hell forever."

"You won. You got all the money. Why can't you forgive him?"

"I'll never forgive him. I would give all the money away if I could have five minutes with him to tell him what I really thought of him."

"I just saw him on the TV," Ruby said.

"Sure you did; they've been flashing his pictures all day on the news." Jenny threw herself on the couch.

Ruby turned to her and said, "Not his picture, Mom. I saw him in line at registration."

Jenny looked at her crossly and demanded, "You using again?"

Ruby ignored her and went over to an envelope that lay discarded on the coffee table. "Let's go." She pulled out two complimentary tickets that had been sent to honor his widow and his only child.

Jenny made a face, coupled with an unladylike snort. "Uh…no. I don't think so."

"Well, I'm going." Ruby raced up the stairs to get dressed. She wanted to be among people who had loved her father.

When she came downstairs, her mother had on makeup and a new outfit. "I might as well go with you. I am the widow of the king, after all." She laughed, finishing her drink. "I will bask in his glory." She bowed unsteadily.

Ruby picked up her phone and dialed work. "I'm not going to be able to come in tonight," she told the manager. She didn't know why, but she felt herself being drawn to the Mandalay.

* * *

Ginny flicked on the television, her face crumpling when she realized it was the registration for the Series. Ramona Heart was in the middle of an interview. She and Ramona had often had drinks while they watched Clutch play. Ramona "Black Widow" Heart was one of the friendlier players. She had an annual Christmas party that included everyone, even nasty players like the Ant. *May he rot in hell,* she thought. A VIP ticket lay on the coffee table—her invitation to reconnect with old friends. The organizer, a buddy of Clutch's, had called and even offered to pick her up. Stan was going to be there. Talk about awkward. She was conflicted. She liked Stan; he was…nice, so easy. Maybe she should let go.

She had just finished filling out registration forms for the culinary school with Ruby's information. She applied for a full scholarship and was placing it in a large manila envelope to mail. *Ruby deserves a chance,* she thought. She'd always liked her.

Ginny switched over to Food Network. They were doing a piece on Stan's barbecue restaurants. She liked Stan. He was much easier than Clutch ever was—peaceful and calm. She knew he was a whale, as they called it in Vegas, one of the big players. That's how they had met—she was subbing as a dealer at a craps tourney at the Wynn. He'd tried to sweep her off her feet with flowers and dinners, but her heart wasn't ready. It still felt like a big, raw bruise. Clutch, for all his charm, had never once told her he loved her. She tried not to be bitter. He had been her life. There was just something about Clutch that made her not think about anything else. She'd had a life before him—friends, trips back to the Philippines, a side career at a nail salon. She had given everything up to devote all her time to Clutch. He was high maintenance but so much fun. He had a way of changing everything into a celebration. And talk about the perks! Her picture was in *People* magazine once when Clutch was named a person to watch in 2004. But on the other hand, Stan didn't even care about her mismatched caps. Some of her teeth were ivory, and the new ones were too white. *That's what happens when you let students do dental work*. They were roasting a whole pig on the show—Stan was demonstrating his new recipe. She smiled. He said it was based on one given to him by a good friend from the Philippines, where they know how to cook perfect pork. He even called it Ginny's Genuine Good Barbecue. She smiled wistfully. He was a good man, but her finger pressed the return on the remote to go back to the poker station.

She recognized so many of the players; my, how she missed them. Oh, they had all come around in the beginning, but as time wore on, life went back to normal for everyone but her. She could almost hear Clutch's voice saying, "It's Clutchtime!" All of his old friends and competitors were there. Ginny's heart ached for the loss of him...or maybe it was the comfort of their old routines. Looking around her barren home, she missed hearing his commentary, his curses; she missed his friendship. She walked over to his empty urn, hugging it close to her chest. Tears pricking her eyes, she remembered the excitement of the first day of the event. Ginny picked up the phone and called in sick to work. She picked up the VIP pass and stuffed it in her purse. First, she would drop off the application at the Culinary Institute, and then she would head to the Series. It was the closest she could get to Clutch and what was familiar right now.

* * *

Harriet Martin screamed, her hands covering her face. Frank ran into the room, a fork in one hand, yellow yolk dripping from his chin. "What's the matter?" he asked worriedly.

She pointed to the screen, her face white. "Trouble, trouble, trouble."

"What?" He looked around the room.

"Telly was there."

Frank looked at the television, shrugging. "Where?"

"At the Poker Series. I saw him. He's there and he's going to play!" she wailed.

Frank pulled the paper napkin from under his neck. "Good for him!"

"You can't mean that," Harriet turned to him, shock on her face.

"Everybody should get a chance to live his dream, at least once. This I gotta see. Call up and get tickets. We're going to watch in person."

CHAPTER NINETEEN

"He's threatening to haunt us for the rest of our lives," Telly pleaded with her. He had come home and broken the news to her hours ago. It felt like they'd been arguing for days. At first, she'd sat silently. Then she had broken out into great, gulping sobs. She'd refused to talk, but Telly had followed her around and wouldn't give up. Finally, he'd tried to convince her about Clutch.

"A ghost, Telly?" Gretchen was crying. "You lied to me. You said you wouldn't play poker anymore."

"You think I *want* to do this?" Telly was incredulous. "We went over it. I have never lied to you, Gretchen."

She shook her head. "I don't want to talk about this anymore."

"Thick..." Telly said wistfully.

Gretchen ignored him and went back to her suitcase on the bed. "I think...I think we need to take a break from each other." She looked up at him, her face filled with shock and hurt. "You lied to me, Telly. You lied."

"What? No, please don't go."

"I love you, Telly, but this is tearing us apart. You have to decide what is more important: me or poker."

"You know the answer to that. It's always you. I love you."

"The sad thing is, I *do* know that. But you are an addict. I have more things to worry about than what makes you happy, Telly." Gretchen paused to look up at him. "I have lived my whole life running from my mother's addictions. I can't do that to—"

"To what?" Telly asked.

Gretchen shook her head. "It ruined my childhood. Don't you see, Telly? I can't let another one ruin what's left for me. It's in your hands. You decide."

"I…I don't have a choice." He took her hand, rubbing the spot that had once had a diamond ring. "Please know that everything I'm doing is for the two of us."

Great, crystal tears ran from Gretchen's sad eyes. *The two of us,* she thought. *Soon to be three,* but the words couldn't escape from her clogged throat. "Don't look for me, Telly. This time you won't find me." He started to go after her and she turned, her face set with determination. "Stop. Don't follow me. I mean it."

She tucked Sophie under her arm and quietly let herself out the door.

Telly sat forlornly on the bed, his eyes smarting.

"You did this," he howled.

"We have a deal, pal. You get the ring; I get the bracelet." Clutch materialized.

"What good is a ring if Gretchen is gone?"

"She'll be back." Clutch sat on the bed. "Once you get your hands on all that money, don't you worry, she'll be back."

"Gretchen isn't like that. She doesn't care about money."

Clutch waved his hand with disgust. "That's a crock. They all care about the money. Now go shower and get ready; we leave in an hour."

"And if I don't?" Telly asked mutinously.

"Unlike you, I know where Gretchen is going. I will find her and take her little ass and—"

Telly launched himself off the bed to attack the ghost, who vanished with a maniacal laugh. "You talked a good game about choices, Telly. Too bad you don't have any."

CHAPTER TWENTY

Telly changed his clothes, his heart heavy in his chest.

"You going to hold up your end of the bargain?" Clutch demanded.

"Like you said, what choice do I have?" Telly's mood was dark.

"Well aren't you a ray of sunshine. What happened to happy Telly?"

Telly walked out the door without answering. He made it to the convention center a half hour later, and while he knew Clutch was there, he was surprised that the ghost was strangely quiet.

The place was packed; the air tingled with excitement and gelled with anticipation. Clusters of people formed while they waited to be placed at tables. There were so many entrants that they couldn't fit them all in one room. Telly was assigned to the second ballroom. Somehow he felt a change in the atmosphere, and he knew Clutch's feathers had been ruffled.

"What is it?" he asked sullenly, looking at Clutch.

Clutch's voice sounded strained. "Look what the cat dragged in," he said.

"What?"

"My murderer. The *pissant*."

"Him?" Telly asked, looking at last year's winner. He was being escorted by an entourage of people. He still wore the same gray hoodie. "He looks much taller on TV," Telly said as Adam "the Ant" Antonowski brushed past him.

The Ant paused to look at Telly, his eyes narrowing. He approached him. "What's your name?" He stood too close to Telly, and even though his nose only came up to Telly's chin, it was unnerving. His squinty eyes measured Telly, and then he smiled, his tiny teeth like mashed chicklets. Telly noticed that his face sported a light peach fuzz instead of a beard. He was young.

"Telly Martin." Telly held out his hand, but the Ant ignored him contemptuously.

"Never heard of you." The Ant's eyes narrowed even more as the younger man dismissed Telly, deciding he was not a threat.

"Tell him that he will," Clutch hissed. The Ant cocked his head, deep in thought, his face turning in Clutch's direction as if he'd heard the ghost speak. Telly wondered if he could see Clutch or maybe sense his presence, but the kid's face registered nothing; it was devoid of emotion.

Telly felt the tension between the two men. The room was thick with hatred and unfilled dreams. Suddenly, the anger drained from Telly, making him feel lighter. He knew Clutch was next to him, the ghost's hurt and diminished confidence pooling around them like a deep puddle. Clutch was a bully—of that there was no doubt—but he had been forced into that life from the cold and calculated attacks against him. He understood Clutch and his need to win. He was minimized by this kid as much as Telly was by other people in his life. All he ever wanted was to succeed, to make people happy, but he was surrounded by negative people who tried to make him into a nothing, from the guy in 4A to Rob Couts. The Ant looked down his snub nose at Telly. He felt his body enveloped by Clutch, as though they were one person. A shield of unity formed between them. His skin prickled with awareness that Clutch was protecting him—he knew it was as new and raw a feeling for the ghost as it was for him. The breath escaped from his lips in a rush, but he felt empowered, strangely safe. A lifetime of disappointment, responsibility, and the need to please all contracted into a small, hard ball and lodged in Telly's chest. *We are all the same,* he thought with astonishment. *Everybody has an "Ant" in their lives. What gives anyone the right to make someone feel less of a person?*

"You will," Telly called after his opponent, knowing already that it would come down to the two of them in the end.

The Ant gave him a hard look and shook his head. "Don't see it happening," he said with a smirk and walked away.

"And there you have it, folks," a heavyset bald man followed the Ant with a microphone. "The reigning champion is setting boundaries and letting everyone know he has no intention of letting a victory slip through his fingers."

Telly felt strangely empty. He knew Clutch had separated from him. Tension sizzled like electricity in the space between them.

"I'm gonna take every one of those chips and shove 'em right where the sun don't shine," Clutch whispered evilly. Despite his heavy heart, Telly smiled. "I know you like me, Telly," Clutch told him.

Telly shook his head. "Nope." The moment was over. His mind had returned to Gretchen and his problems there.

"Yes, you do, and by the time we finish, you're gonna admit I was the best thing that ever happened to you," Clutch said confidently.

CHAPTER TWENTY ONE

"Thanks for letting me crash here," Gretchen said sadly. She was dressed in a nightgown in Chrissy's spare bedroom. "You're sure Jack won't mind?"

"Forget about him; he moved out yesterday. Want to talk about what happened with you and Telly?"

Gretchen shook her head and asked, "Did you two have a fight?"

"Nope." Chrissy lit a cigarette, inhaling deeply. "It was just time to move on." Her face brightened with a snide smile. "Telly's on television, you know." Chrissy sat down on the bed.

"You saw him again?" Gretchen's face lit up.

"Yeah, every time the camera pans the room, it catches him."

"How did he look?"

"Nervous. You want to see?"

Gretchen's cell rang. It was Harriet, Telly's mother. She looked at her phone, not wanting to, but answered it anyway.

"Gretchen! I thought it was out of his system," Harriet's shrill voice said.

Gretchen shrugged. Harriet repeated her name with insistence. Gretchen began with a heartfelt sigh. "I don't know what came over him. He was crazy." Gretchen winced when she said that. "How did you find out?"

"He's on the television. What's wrong with him?" Harriet spoke so loudly that the people in the next house could probably hear her. Gretchen heard Frank's muffled voice, asking questions. Harriet shushed him. "I asked that already!"

"I…I don't know. I don't know what's wrong with him."

"Where are you? Do you want us to come and get you?" Harriet asked, her voice worried.

"I'm all right. I have to think. Look, I'll call you tomorrow." She turned to Chrissy and said, "Turn it on. Let me see."

Two men in light blue sport coats sat at a desk, a large monitor behind them. "A record two rooms again this year, Kevin. Almost twelve thousand players."

"I know, Stu. New faces. New money. It's anybody's game this year."

"The one person we *won't* be seeing will be poker legend Clutch Henderson, who sadly passed away last year."

"And now, the poker world will hold a sixty-second vigil for our beloved Clutch," the announcer's voice intoned. The newscasters bowed their heads respectfully.

The crowd lowered their heads. Gretchen stood, coming closer to the screen. She spotted Telly staring into space, his head cocked to one side. He was worried. She looked at him…really looked at him, concern mirrored in her own expression. His eyes were troubled, his lips firm. He spotted the camera zooming in on his face, his indigo eyes changing. It was as if he knew she was watching. It was something special between them, as if they could sense each other all the time. His eyes softened, and she knew without a doubt that he was aware that she was looking at him. He touched his lips, and she saw him mouth the word *thick*.

He needed her. She started getting dressed.

"Where are you going?" Chrissy asked.

"I'm going to Telly. To the tournament." Gretchen turned green, put her hand over her mouth, and ran to the bathroom, retching up everything she had eaten in the last twenty-four hours.

"You won't get far like that," Chrissy told her, her phone in her hand. "Let me call someone who can give you a ride."

CHAPTER TWENTY TWO

"Bunch of two-faced phonies," Clutch said as he walked around, looking at his former colleagues. "You think a sixty-second vigil is going to keep my memory alive? I'll show each and every one of you money-hungry bastards what it's like to lose, and there ain't nothing you can do about it."

He walked between the tight rows, tapping a head here, pinching a face there. Telly was the only witness to his commentary. "This here is Miguel the Mantis. He sits so quietly he blends in with the furniture, and you never see it coming when he gets you. Black Widow…" He bent over to kiss the cheek of Ramona Heart, the woman Telly had played with at the Mirage. "Tel, she's a real black widow—six or seven guys she's been married to. Lucky Leroy." He pumped an imaginary handshake with another player and then knocked off his cap. "Only real hats should be allowed. Why do they wear these sissy head coverings?" He leaned close, making eye contact with the oblivious person. "This is not de rigueur in the Old West or even the New West. You city boys look like ass-holes." He skipped through the narrow aisles, his acerbic commentary describing the personalities of the players hilarious. Telly laughed out loud at his ghostly antics.

* * *

Gretchen peered closely at the television set while she dressed. "What's he laughing at?"

"He looks demented," Chrissy said helpfully.

Gretchen shook her head. "No. He's talking to someone. Look. His eyes are following someone. Who did you get to give me a lift?"

"You're as nuts as he is. He's laughing like an idiot!"

"He's not an idiot!" Gretchen scanned the space where Telly was looking. No help there…she saw nothing. "I have to leave; Telly needs me."

"Crazy is as crazy does. I wouldn't give him the time of day."

"I know Telly. Something is going on."

The camera came in for an extreme close-up of his face. The announcer chuckled and said, "I wonder what he thinks is so funny. Strange guy—do you know his name?"

"Look, he's saying something into the camera," Kevin observed.

Telly blew a kiss, mouthing, "I'm sorry, Gretchen. I love you." He touched his hand over his heart.

Gretchen's insides turned liquid. Balling her fists, she punched the bed impotently. "I don't know why I got so mad." She watched, her eyes going wide when she saw his shirt being pulled by an invisible hand. "Look at that,"

Gretchen said, moving closer. "There's nobody behind him."

Telly reached behind him, slapping the unseen hands. "He really thinks he's being haunted." Gretchen picked up her purse.

"Your ride is here," Chrissy said as she looked out the window.

"You didn't," Gretchen accused her, seeing the Firebird.

"I did, and you better hurry. He's playing and said he can't be late."

Gretchen worried her bottom lip. Outside, Rob Couts pressed the horn with a loud blast.

"If you're going to rescue that loser, you better leave. Rob will get you in; he's got a parking pass." Chrissy pushed her out the door. "Go, already."

"I don't want to go with him," Gretchen whimpered.

Chrissy held the door open; Gretchen stood frozen on the landing. "Stop being a baby. If you want to get to Telly, just go already. Oh, don't worry about Rob. We started dating last night. You're safe."

Gretchen slid into the interior of Rob's car silently. She nodded. "You're playing in the Series?" she asked timidly.

Rob didn't answer. He pulled away from the curb sharply, knowing his muscles bulged nicely under his short-sleeve T-shirt.

They jumped onto the highway. "The little guy playing?" he asked.

"He's not little, and yes, he is."

"He won't last long," Rob said confidently.

Gretchen bristled. The fact was, she also believed that Telly wouldn't last long. He was too trusting, and he was not a good judge of character. Still, all of a sudden her anger and resentment simply vanished. *You can't penalize a guy for being good,* she thought. Telly thought he was protecting them. Even if it wasn't real, his intent was good. She felt shame steal over her face. "Telly will win. I feel it in my heart. He will play well today."

Rob cupped his balls and said crudely, "Well, I feel right here you're going to be with me by next week."

Gretchen opened the door before they even stopped, getting out. She jumped out without a word. Rob was faster, running around to grip her arm. He pulled her into a tight embrace, one hand holding her head, the other her waist. He kissed her deeply, passionately. The crowd that stood outside the convention center roared with approval. Gretchen, half his size, was captive. A camera crew caught the kiss but not the resounding slap that followed.

* * *

Ruby and Jenny arrived at the convention center, showed their VIP passes, and headed to the exclusive party for guests. Ruby was greeted warmly, Jenny not as much. Old friends surrounded the young girl, exclaiming at how beautiful she was, how much she had changed and grown up…and wouldn't Clutch be proud. Jenny hit the bar and picked at the seafood on display, craning her neck for someone, anyone, to talk to. Jenny was de trop; although she knew most of the guests and had partied with them while she was married, even vacationed with them in exotic locales for the poker tourneys, they virtually ignored her. It was as if they'd divorced her when the marriage had ended. *Hey,* she wanted to shout, *I'm still married to the bastard.* The more she drank, the angrier she got. Soon the room moved as if she were on a rocky ship, and somehow her speech didn't seem clear, her words confused. They avoided her like she had a communicable disease. "I'm rich now, you stupid bastards," she grumbled. "I got it all, and don't think I don't know how to use it. I'm not going to gamble it away." A commotion by the entrance drew her attention. She spied a happy cluster around Ginny, Clutch's girlfriend. She was hugged and ushered to a table, where they treated her like the grieving widow, getting her drinks and food for comfort. Some held her hand, and others put their arms around her shoulders, tears in their eyes. Her stupid kid moved close to the fat pig, linking arms like a mother and daughter. *Hey, that's my kid; get your own.* She must have said it out loud because a space cleared around her, and a hush came over the room. Jenny glared at her former friends, and her rage intensified—fueled by jealousy and nurtured with hatred—finally boiling over when Ginny wiped lipstick tenderly from Ruby's cheek.

Jenny stalked over, her eyes dark slivers of heat, her fists balled. "You have your nerve showing up here!" Conversations stopped completely, and the room grew quiet.

"I had an invitation." Ginny told her.

"Who'd you sleep with to get it?" Jenny spat.

"Mom!" Ruby wailed.

Ginny shook her head and with quiet dignity said, "Clutch."

Jenny threw her cocktail at Ginny. Casino cameras dispatched security to escort Jenny from the room. "Are you coming with me?" she demanded from her daughter.

Ruby wiped Ginny's arm with a napkin; she wouldn't look at her mother. She shook her head. "I'm staying."

"I'll be at the crap tables." She shook off the guards. "I can play at the crap tables, right?" she asked contemptuously. The guard looked at the host, who assented. Jenny took one last look at her daughter and said, "Don't forget who you came with, and don't forget who holds the key to all your money."

She walked out, and Ruby looked up at Ginny. "I don't care about the money. I miss my dad."

Ginny cupped her cheek. "We all do, honey. Let's go eat some cake."

* * *

"What do you mean we can't get in?" Harriet demanded, her face beet red. She stamped her feet like a spoiled child.

The guard wearily shook his head. "Sorry, ma'am. You need tickets."

"How do we get them?" Frank calmly asked after putting a hand on his wife's arm.

"Give him something, Frank. Maybe he'll let us in. Give him five dollars." She spoke as if he wasn't there listening to them.

"I'm sorry, ma'am. I can't take any money. You are allowed, however, to go into the casino and watch on the big screens."

Harriet steamed up like a hot teapot, but Frank grabbed her hand and headed to the entrance. "It'll have to do."

* * *

A film crew moved through the casino with determination. Georgia Oaken walked with a smile, stopping players to tell them she was a medium and would do a spot reading. Stan waited for her outside the designated spot for his prearranged session. A small group of people stood in line. The producer came over and explained how the reading would proceed. Stan was first.

A young girl wearing a headset attached to her ear, no older than his granddaughter, led him inside to a table on a dais. The room had been decorated with candles circling an intimate black-draped table in the center of the room. Taking out her sage, Georgia lit it, laughing. "Wow, I never expected to see so many spirits here."

Stan was nervous. He placed his hat on a chair behind him. He liked Ginny. How would Irma take it? Could you love two women at the same time?

Scribbling on a pad, Georgia looked up, her startling black eyes merry. "She's a pip, this person. What does the number forty-two mean to you?"

Stan swallowed and then cleared his throat. "We were married forty-two years."

"Hummm. It was a happy marriage. She said she rolled the dice on you and won. I've never had a craps reference; does that have significance?"

Stan nodded, his mouth dry. He had to admit he'd entered this reading as a skeptic. Two for two were good odds, he calculated. This Georgia might just be the real deal.

"She calls out to your kids. She calls you all a *hard eight*—I don't know what she means."

"It's a craps reference. We have six kids. We used to call our family the Hard Eights."

Georgia put her hand on her chest, her breathing a bit labored. "I'm having trouble breathing. Did she die from a breathing issue?"

"Lung cancer."

Georgia nodded with understanding. "She's telling me to tell you she's breathing fine now." She cocked her head, the diffused light softening the shock of her black-and-white hair. "OK…I don't know what this means, but she says, 'I'm moving over; there's room for one more.'"

Stan nodded silently. He worried about their graves. They were supposed to be buried together. He loved Ginny too. Did he have to choose who he was to spend eternity with?

"She wants you to know that she had the best life. *Is* having the best life. It hasn't ended for her. She doesn't want it to end for you either; do you understand that?"

"I think so…I'm not sure," Stan stuttered.

Georgia laughed. "She says that after forty years you should know exactly what she means. Go out and ask your new friend to come home with you again. This time she will probably say yes."

Stan sat back stunned, his eyes smarting. Georgia went on, "Your wife gave a beautiful session that was filled with love. She wants you to feel love here and now. She's a pretty strong soul, and if that's what she's telling you to do, I wouldn't mess with her."

Georgia looked up to find that Stan was already gone.

* * *

"Something is going on there," Harriet said through a crammed mouth. She had a hotdog in one hand and a piña colada in the other. "Frank, go find out what happened." She pushed him with her elbow. Frank handed her his giant buttered pretzel. Harriet took it gingerly. "You're getting butter everywhere. Go—never mind." Harriet went toward the bar to get napkins.

There was a commotion at the craps tables. Police were everywhere. A woman stood, her legs apart, her hands cuffed behind her back.

A pit boss was holding a pair of dice. He took one die between two fingers and held it up to the light. "See," he told the uniformed cop, "if you hold it right." Then he turned to the young girl nervously moving from foot to foot on the sidelines. "Ruby, you can't be here. You know the rules. Ginny!" he called to Clutch's girlfriend. "Take her off the floor."

The officer gave her a stern look. Ginny herded Ruby toward the poker tournament rooms. He looked at the weighted dice. "I can see the weights. Cheating is a serious offense." He looked down at her license. "Ms. Henderson."

"Clutch would die if he saw this, Jenny. Why?" asked the pit boss.

"Blow it out your ass, Phil," she said. She pivoted on wobbly legs to the police officer. "They switched the dice. I would never play with those."

The officer took her by the arm. "Yeah, yeah. Let's go."

CHAPTER TWENTY THREE

The screen settled on the two announcers again. "OK, folks, let's wheel them and deal them."

The camera zoomed in on a dealer's hands as he started dealing out the cards. There was a feeling of anticipation in the room, a great hum building in volume that sounded like the roar of a revving engine. Hands were eager, bets were made, and the games began.

The afternoon went on, evening turned to night, and slowly the crowded tables thinned and were condensed into new tables. The group morphed, and tension built, the sounds ebbing and flowing as the atmosphere changed. Screams of triumph mixed with moans of defeat as people were eliminated. It was clear who the victors were by the increasing mountain of chips accumulated. Occasionally, someone had to be led away, his or her curses echoing in the exit corridor. The movement of losers leaving was a constant stream, their shoulders hunched with dejection, their faces lined with defeat. The steady thrum and murmur of the game was occasionally interrupted by a random outburst of applause as chip leaders were identified. The camera constantly made guesswork of who would be left, and more times than not landed on Telly's rapt face. Telly never looked at his opponents; he didn't want to get to know them. He didn't realize that Rob Couts was playing around him—his goal was to end up at Telly's table.

"Who is that guy?" Kevin asked.

"Never seen him before." Stu held the mike. "Ramona 'Black Widow' Heart is here. How'd you do, Ramona?"

The woman who'd played in the Mirage with Telly earlier that week leaned forward to speak into the proffered mike. "Not as good as I hoped. Got taken out by a flush early in the game." She shook her head, her dark mole prominent on her cheek. "Kinda snuck up on me."

"The flush?"

"No, Telly 'No Tells.'" She pointed vaguely to the vast room filled with hundreds of games.

"Who?" Kevin searched the floor.

"That guy over there. Came onto the scene like a ghost. Never seen anything like him."

"Really? Tell us about him," Kevin said.

"That's the point—you can't. He gives nothing away. No facial expressions, no tics. I never saw that flush coming."

"Went all in?"

"You bet. I had a straight. Everybody's got something. I plan on keeping my eye on that guy."

"Well, thanks for the heads up, Ramona. So what's next in your life?"

"I'm going to try my luck on the European circuit for a while. Change of scenery, change of luck," she said with a smile.

"Good luck with Europe, and we'll see you back here for the start of the new season at the Reno Invitational. Now let's take a little look at Telly 'No Tells.'" The camera zoomed in to watch Telly, who sat impassively, his face neutral.

"Raise him!" Clutch slapped Telly on the top of his head. At this point, Telly was running on no sleep and felt like an automaton. Nothing Clutch did fazed him. "He's got jack shit." Clutch pranced around to a fellow with long braids and a Native American scout hat. He was known as Simon the Prophet. "You think you're gonna raise me with a chasing flush and get away with it? Telly, reraise this dumbass now!"

Telly stared bleakly at his hold cards, which confirmed he had trip queens. He liked this player and hated to see him forced out. The Prophet was one of the good guys—always playing for charity. Telly didn't want to be the cause of his losing. He cut out five million dollars from his enormous pile but hesitated, his fingers fiddling with the top chip.

"What are you waiting for? Move in for the kill," Clutch ordered.

Telly licked his lips with indecision. It didn't feel right. He sunk low, his head dipping between his shoulder blades. He looked at all the other players who were staring at him as if he were going to pounce at any minute. The fear he saw in their eyes shocked him. They were afraid of him. *How odd,* he thought. As if he wanted to or even could hurt anybody. So this was what it was like being one of the cool guys. The novelty of gambling and the quest for that elusive win wore off with the impact of a freight train. The breadth of that realization left Telly in a rush. He smiled tentatively to all the players who were sitting in mute agony over his next move. This didn't feel good.

"You're not thinking of doing what I think you're thinking!" Clutch jumped onto the table. "You bleeding, stupid-ass heart! He cheats on his wife! He's not a goody-two-shoes," Clutch screamed.

Telly calmly threw in his cards, folding.

"What? You idiot. You had it all. The Prophet should be walking the walk of shame right now. He played dumb! What's the matter with you?" Light dawned on Clutch's face when he realized Telly's plan. "You're going to let it all go, aren't you?"

Telly nodded imperceptibly, a vague smile on his face.

"You think I'm gonna let you walk out of here when we are so close?" Clutch was leaning down, sending blasts of freezing air down Telly's back. He shivered. "Yeah, you better shiver. It's not just me staring daggers at you, loser. That guy can't wait to take you down." Clutch was pointing to another player two tables away. Telly wouldn't look. Clutch grabbed his face with icy fingers, forcing him to look in the opposite direction. Telly gave in gracelessly, his eyes focusing on a bald head with black, bullet eyes staring with hatred at him.

"Rob Couts," Telly whispered under his breath.

Rob caught his eye, pointing his finger as if it were a gun at Telly. He made a soft noise as though he were shooting. Telly felt the impact of his intent. He squirmed in his seat, Clutch's mouth hovering near his ear. "He wants to take you out, Tel. He's dying to show everybody you're a nothing. You gonna let that happen?"

Telly anted up for the next game. He was back in.

* * *

Gretchen pushed her way inside the convention center. Sitting in the rear, she was sandwiched between poker geeks, guys with MacBooks, and avid fans. Of Telly there was no sign. The fact that she'd made it in there at all was a miracle in itself. The smell of food hit her nostrils, making her mouth water. The nausea was sudden; her knees went weak. Gretchen staggered to the ladies' room and, instead of watching Telly, she watched the water circle clockwise in the toilet bowl. *Some help I turned out to be,* she thought miserably.

* * *

A tall, angular man sat down at Telly's table. "I'm going to skin you alive..." he said. The voice was so familiar. Telly tried to place him, but he couldn't until he finished with, "...loser."

"Do I know you?" Telly asked.

"It's the thief from 4A." Clutch came up from behind him. "You better take this bastard down."

"In a blaze of glory." Telly felt adrenaline course through his body. He bounced his leg with anticipation.

"Who you talking to, loser?"

"You." Telly looked up, his eyes lit with determination. He looked off to the side and winked.

"There he goes again," a woman wearing a tight shirt, her boobs exposed for all and sundry, said to the table. But what did it all mean? No one knew.

After playing just three hands, 4A found himself being walked out of the games, making room for another to slide into his place. Telly began to feel like he was playing against anyone who had insulted or made fun of him this week. The revolving door of contestants went up against him, boasting that they would be the ones to take out the rookie, only to leave with their tail between their legs. They underestimated him with cocky confidence, feral leers, and finally outright shock when he eliminated them one by one.

The room had gotten quiet. It was nearing two in the morning. Twenty-eight players were waiting to bag what was left of their chips for the last three tables tomorrow. Only twenty-seven players would move on. Of the 12,000 original contestants, 11,973 had bitten the dust. The big day would start with three tables, reduce to two, and end with the final competitors, who would play for the International Championship. Telly was alternately called the Terminator and No Tells as he knocked out players like a Sherman tank. Everyone was exhausted. Players folded, leaving Telly, Rob Couts, and George "The Gospel" Cantlee, who Clutch was now calling George "Can't See Shit."

"Hi, Radio." Telly recognized the insult in Rob's voice and looked up, bleary-eyed, to find the shiny bald head and bullet eyes of Gretchen's boss filling a seat at his table.

"You know this asshole?" Clutch asked. "He's been watching you all night."

Under his breath Telly grunted, "Rob Couts."

"Cooty Man," Clutch said, his finger deep inside the man's nose. Telly smiled for the first time that evening. He looked at his suited connectors, a ten of spades, and a jack of spades and heard Clutch mutter, "A lot of possibilities."

No shit, Telly thought. He wanted to beat Rob—show him he could play. The flop revealed nine of clubs, queen of spades, and two of spades.

"You have a possible open-ended straight or a flush. Not bad."

Clutch moved behind Rob. He shrugged, his eyes opening wide, when he raised two million dollars. "He's got nothing. Seven-deuce. What the fuck is this guy in for?"

Telly shrugged with one shoulder, met the bet, and watched as the next card pretty much sealed his fate as the winner. He looked up at Rob's evil grin, feeling his face tighten with shame. Cheating was no way to beat some-one. It was wrong.

"Put him outta his misery, Telly. Go all in." Clutch was leaning over the table.

Telly hesitated. His eyes felt heavy. He shuffled his chips and put them down.

"What the…what are you waiting for? Take him out, and you are in the finals room. Do it, moron!"

Telly had had just about enough. He was playing like a marionette, with Clutch at the strings. This wasn't poker; this wasn't sportsmanship—it was a disgrace. All Telly could think about was Gretchen and how he was going to get her back. He half rose. He was sick of Clutch and his abuse. "Don't call me a moron."

"Say what?" Couts looked up from his hand.

"I wasn't talking to you."

"You're crazy. Everybody knows it. You've played at the big-boy tables long enough. I'm going to annihilate you," Rob spat.

"You gonna let him talk to you like you're shit?" Clutch came so close, Telly could feel the cold air that surrounded him. "You're finally acting like a man. You know what they're calling you? Do you?" Clutch screamed. "They're calling you Telly 'No Tells.' You *earned* that. You don't give nothing away. You got here from your stone face."

That was apathy, Telly thought, *not a poker face.*

Clutch responded, even though he hadn't spoken out loud. "Nothing matters but the game. Sit down and, for the first time in your life, finish something. Hey, where you going?" Clutch followed Telly as he abruptly got up and stalked from the table. "Telly, get back in here now!"

"See that?" Rob shouted, pointing to Telly's retreating back. "I faked him out. I did it. Remember my name: Rob Couts. I'm the next champ."

The remaining players all looked at each other with a shrug. "Bathroom?" one of them suggested.

"Who knows. He probably pisses ice water." An older man sat back with relief.

"Ice cubes," a woman said with a smirk.

"Ouch," said the dealer.

"All I know is that I took him out," Rob said triumphantly.

"It's just one game, sonny. He's still chip leader."

Telly stormed into the bathroom, and Clutch followed him into the stall. "What's the matter with you?" Clutch hit him on the forehead. "We're having a good day. A really good day."

"No *we* are not. I can't do this anymore."

"Why?"

"You are burning a hole into my brain," Telly whispered furiously. "I can't listen to you anymore."

"But I'm winning," Clutch whined. "*We're* winning," he corrected.

"I just want you out of my life. I don't want to ever see another card again."

"Stop talking shit, Telly. This is what you wanted."

"But at what cost?" Telly sat down on the toilet seat with defeat.

"Give me your phone," Clutch demanded, holding out his hand.

Telly handed over his iPhone without comment, his head leaning against the cold wall. He was exhausted. All he wanted was to go home and find Gretchen, sit in bed, and eat ice cream.

"You had your chance to take out that two-bit loser. You held the card. You think I'm doing everything? *You're* making the moves; *you're* placing the bets."

"But *you're* telling me what to do!" Telly finished for him.

"So? I'm just evening the playing field. What have scruples done for you?" he demanded, his cold finger poking Telly in the chest. "Watch and learn, grasshopper."

Clutch found what he was looking for on Telly's phone. "This was all over the news this morning."

Telly saw the outside of the convention center earlier that day. The newscaster was doing a story on good-luck charms. Telly watched the parade of feathers, rabbits' feet, lucky socks, hats, and rings.

Then the announcer chuckled and said, "All of that is trumped by the best good-luck charm of them all: the good-luck kiss." Telly felt both his stomach and jaw drop when the camera zoomed in, showing Gretchen lip-locked with Rob Couts. He threw the phone against the wall and watched it shatter against the tile.

"It's just you and me, kid. Just you and me. Let's go out and kick Rob Couts back to the sewer where he belongs."

Telly mechanically washed his face, knowing he was done with feeling, any feeling, and ready to do battle for all the little guys.

* * *

"Tell me something, Mr. Telly 'No Tells.' Tell me I'm the one who finally kicked your skinny ass out of here," Couts taunted.

There was one thing Telly hated more than Clutch, and that was a bully. "I'm all in," Telly said, back in the game once more as the cards came his way. He looked at the three of hearts, five of clubs, and six of clubs, wondering if he'd just kissed the championship away. He heard Clutch speaking but tuned him out. Anger filled his head until all he felt was a driving need to outplay his nemesis, by himself. His face set, Telly looked up at Couts, knowing somehow that the atmosphere had changed between the two of them. Clutch stood nervously, putting his hands on the back of the chair. He was shuffling his feet and stretching his huge arms over his head. Telly watched with steely resolve.

Sweat broke out on Rob's forehead as he considered his cards and looked back at Telly. He pushed his pile into the center. "I'm all in."

Telly exposed his cards, his face impassive. The table murmured with surprise.

"I knew I had you," Rob crowed, showing his pocket queens.

Telly shrugged. Another player defended him, saying, "It's not over yet, Couts."It was clear Telly was fast becoming a favorite.

It didn't look good, and everyone knew it. Telly's two cards were ace of hearts and ten of spades.

"This looks serious, folks. It could be the end of the road for the new guy on the block," Stu predicted as tension mounted.

The turn came and went, with no improvement for Telly.

Kevin whispered, as if his voice could affect the game, "Only an ace can save Telly 'No Tells' at this point."

"Here comes the river! One time!" Clutch yelled.

Telly stood, repeating "One time" like a prayer.

Kevin reported, "Telly just asked for his One Time. And only an ace, as I said before, will save him and send Rob Couts home."

The dealer flipped the card, and the crowd exploded with excitement as an ace of diamonds floated onto the felt.

Couts's jaw dropped, no sound coming out of his mouth.

Telly looked up without a smile. "It's time for you to leave."

"That's what I'm talking about!" Clutch did a Texas two-step around the table, and Telly found himself entering the next phase of the championship as more players were culled.

CHAPTER TWENTY FOUR

"Looks like we have a huge chip leader already, Kevin," Stu said from his spot on the mezzanine in the broadcast center.

"Yup, newcomer to the game Telly 'No Tells' Martin waltzed into the convention center—wait, scratch that—*stormed* into the convention center and has become a chip magnet."

The camera zoomed in on two men alone at a table, both standing. "I call." The Series winner from four years ago squared off on his end of the table. "Come on, baby, gimme hearts," he prayed out loud.

To the left of the room, the rows of chairs formed a gallery for the spectators. It had thinned out except for die-hard poker fans. Reporters stayed in their roped-off section taking notes. There was an ongoing party in an adjoining room, Telly had heard. He knew many of the players' family members were in there watching on large screens. His breath hitched, lodging in his heart at the knowledge that there was no one watching and rooting for him. No one at all.

The dealer turned the next card. The camera panned the room. All attention rested on Telly and the world-class player with whom he was locked in battle. A soft curse filled the silence as another player kissed his chips good-bye.

"Did Telly Martin just knock out Harvey Fishbeck?" Stu asked, his face stunned from the move.

"If I didn't see it with my own eyes, I wouldn't believe it, Stu. He is known as the best player in the world." Kevin was laughing, wiping tears from his eyes.

"I tell you what, you couldn't see anything from the expression on his face. Telly 'No Tells' is right. The man is devoid of emotion," Stu confirmed.

"He has the same look on his face I did when my third wife told me she was leaving. I didn't know what hit me." Keven chuckled.

"Talk about knowing your opponent. Telly Martin is a new force to be reckoned with."

The camera caressed Telly's face. There were already a Twitter account and a Facebook page devoted to his every move, and he didn't even realize it.

"Come on, Telly. Don't be mad at me. Lighten up. We're making real headway. By the way, seat six has a jack-queen." Clutch meandered around the table. "Seat seven here is holding king-four. Seat eight has a pair. Seat nine has...hey, what is it now?"

"I have to go to the bathroom," Telly said, slowly getting to his feet. His knees had locked; he staggered with fatigue. *How could anyone think this is fun?* he thought. Everything hurt.

"I'll alert the press," an older man with an old frayed Dodgers cap on his head said snidely. He took it off and brushed back his comb-over.

Clutch walked ahead of him, bouncing and chattering away. They came around the bend, and both of them stopped cold in their tracks. Gretchen was emerging from the ladies' room, her face white. Ginny stood leaning against the wall, a balled-up tissue in her hand. Ruby stood next to her, rubbing her back.

"Gretchen!" Telly ran forward to hug her. "I'm sorry."

She opened her arms, falling into his embrace. "Telly!" She burst into tears. "I know you're telling the truth. There really is a ghost."

"I would never lie to you." He pressed his face next to her head.

"Neither would I." She kissed him full on the lips.

Clutch turned, his face nasty. "All right then. Ask her why she swapped spit with Cooty Man."

Telly shook his head. "I don't care if she kissed Rob."

"Telly, let me explain," she said urgently.

"You don't have to, Gretch. I'm good at reading people, and there's no one I like reading more than you."

She pulled him down for another kiss, but before their lips touched, she whispered, "Thick."

Telly didn't have the words to respond. He showed her.

Gretchen rested her head against his chest and said, "Telly, I have to tell you something."

"Later. I have to get back. If I don't finish, he'll never leave us alone. All I want is to be alone with you."

Clutch made gagging noises. He turned to Ginny, "Are you watching this, Gin? Is it making you as sick as it's making me? Looking good, baby. I missed you."

Ginny and Ruby watched the other couple. "I think he's the chip leader." Ginny gestured to Telly.

"If Dad was here, he wouldn't be," Ruby said as they linked arms.

"That's m'girl," Clutch said proudly. He placed his arm around Ginny. "I'd like to catch up with you, babe, but I got a lot to do."

"You know," Ginny said to Ruby, "I thought it would hurt more coming here today."

"Me too," Ruby agreed.

Clutch stopped well, *dead*, in his tracks. He paused to listen to them, his face changing from confidence to hurt.

"Yes, it's like a chapter is closing." Ginny had a dreamy smile on her face as they walked toward the exit. "I spoke to Stan. You'll come with us. He's going to give you a spot to apprentice in one of his restaurants. In the fall, you'll come back for the culinary institute, if they accept you."

"Oh, I'm going to make it." Their voices faded as they left the corridor.

"Hey, now!" Clutch felt an emptiness envelop him. He spied the white-haired angel leaning against the wall. "What are you doing here?" he asked grumpily.

"You snooze, you lose."

"What's that supposed to mean?" Clutch followed Sten as he walked down the hallway toward the convention center.

"Figure it out for yourself," Sten responded as he disappeared.

Clutch saw Ginny and Ruby walking toward the poker room. If he'd had a breath, it would have left him with a *whoosh*. "Ginny…" he sighed.

"What's he like?" Gretchen whispered as she looked around the hallway. The fluorescent lights left nothing to the imagination, but she still looked for strange, moving shadows.

"He's back there, moping," Telly said as he pointed behind him. "It's like being with a Yosemite Sam cartoon on repeat."

Gretchen giggled. Telly looked down at her pretty face. It was almost three in the morning. Her mascara had run and her hair was sticky with God only knew what, but Telly thought she was the most beautiful girl on earth. He cupped her face and whispered, "Thin…I got to go. Try to get in the front. It won't be long now, and we can go home for a few hours."

"Oh, get a room already," Clutch said, standing next to them.

Gretchen pulled away from Telly. "Is he near us?"

"Practically on top of us."

"I mean it—get a room. They'll comp you one. We have to be on our A game tomorrow," Clutch said.

"Let me go and finish this game, and then we'll get out of here." He walked toward the entrance to the poker room. "Wish me luck."

"You don't need it. I'll be waiting."

CHAPTER TWENTY FIVE

Telly did indeed ask for a room. He and Gretchen spent the night in the hotel. The hotel phone rang early, Kevin Franklyn's voice coming through the receiver.

"Did I wake you?" the announcer asked.

Telly sat up, rubbing his eyes. "No, not really—um, yes, you did. Who is this?"

"Kevin Franklyn. I was hoping to do an interview with you before they set up the final three tables."

Telly reached over for his watch. "What time?"

"Half hour."

"It's going to be more like an hour." Telly hung up.

"You're in the big time now." Clutch was sitting on the dresser.

Telly jumped and then quickly covered Gretchen, who sleepily murmured it was cold.

"One more day and we call it quits." Telly rose to go to the bathroom. "Twenty-four hours, and if I never hear the name Clutch Henderson again—"

Clutch moved his fingers and thumb as though it were a mouth talking. "Blah, blah, blah, you know you are having the time of your life." The door slammed in his face.

***

A hand came down hard on his shoulder. "Hi, Telly. Kevin Franklyn." He held out a hand to shake warmly. "This won't take long."

Telly was holding Gretchen's elbow. She was pulled aside; a mike was attached to his shirt; and he was led to a raised dais.

"We are here with Telly Martin, now being called Telly 'No Tells.' Telly is the chip leader at this year's main event. Telly…"—he leaned forward as if they were sharing a confidence—"What's your strategy?"

Telly looked up thoughtfully. "Well, Kevin, thank you for the insightful question. I ha…really have a good read on all my opponents."

"Yes." Clearly, Kevin was expecting more.

"I um…well, I am very good at reading…um, tics from the other players. You know, at the table."

"You OK there, Telly? You look a little pale," Kevin asked.

"Didn't sleep much." They shared a chuckle. Telly winked at Gretchen, who blushed prettily off camera.

"We've never really seen you before. How long have you been playing?"

"Roughly…"—Telly paused as if to count—"…three months."

"Three months? Really." Kevin was shocked. "Sounds like you are a prodigy. Do you have anything you want to say to anyone out there?"

"My fiancée, Gretchen." Telly looked directly into the camera, his face earnest. "I have only one thing to say… through thick and thin." He pointed to the region over his heart.

"Well, there you have it, folks. The brightest star on the poker horizon is landing right here and lighting up the Sixty-sixth Annual International Series of Poker."

* * *

"Two kings! Raise with your aces!" Clutch screamed, his voice rusty from yesterday's marathon. Methodically, players left the table as Telly amassed a huge pile of chips.

"If there is one word that dominated this year's tournament, Kev, that word would be *Telly.*"

"He's like the Rain Man of poker—just look at him. He's a genius. I wonder if the Ant is feeling the strain." The announcers continued their commentary.

They were down to the final two tables, but already, half the players were eliminated. Telly looked up to find the Ant watching him with a hard stare.

"We're coming to the end here, and I can't wait to see if those two pups, No Tells and the Ant, end up going head to head," Kevin said.

"Sounds like a Disney movie!" They both laughed.

In the gallery Stan sat, his arm around Ginny and Ruby on his other side. They had spent the night in the hotel as well, staying to watch the end of the tournament. Ruby had no one to go home to. Jenny was still in jail, with no chance of bail. She had bitten a policewoman and was now on psychiatric watch.

Harriet and Frank had spent the night at home and returned, though they were still on the outside. They had made friends with a host who had not only allowed them to sit in the high-roller lounge to watch but also comped them lunch at the buffet.

Gretchen sat front and center, her eyes never leaving Telly.

"Fold!" Clutch shouted.

Telly folded without any emotion, looking at his pile of thirty million in chips. *Won't be much longer now; this charade should end soon,* he thought eagerly.

"Bet a million," Clutch ordered. Robotically, he bet a boatload of chips. "Reraise." The orders came in rapid fire. Telly was stunned that he had gotten this far. Half the time, he didn't even know what he was doing. "Check!"

"I'm gonna bet." The guy with the baseball cap and comb-over was still here. He was known as Fat Bastard East, as opposed to Fat Bastard West, who had been knocked out of the game hours before.

"Raise 'em, raise 'em now," Clutch whispered.

"I fold," Telly laid his cards down. He had a shit hand. It was stupid to waste chips. For the first time, something clicked. He trusted his own judgment rather than Clutch's. "You don't know what you're doing," Telly said out loud.

"Like hell you're going to fold—who do you think you are?" Clutch whispered fiercely.

"Watch me," Telly stated with finality.

"Are you talking to me?" Fat Bastard East asked. "Because I don't know what in the hell you are talking about."

"Your card then," the dealer said to Telly. "Are you in or out?"

"Nooooo!" Clutch jumped on the table.

"Yes!" Telly said.

Clutch gripped Telly's hand, wrestling with the cards. Telly tried to force a fold, but Clutch bent the cards backward over his hand. Telly's lips turned white with the effort of fighting Clutch's death grip on his wrist. The cards flew across the table, hitting Fat Bastard East in the eye.

Telly jumped up and apologized. The room erupted into clapping, whistling, and cheers. Clearly, Fat Bastard East was not a popular player.

Pandemonium broke out. Fat Bastard East rose, taking a swing at Telly. Immediately they were separated, and peace was restored. Once it was determined that there was no damage to Fat Bastard East's eye, the next game began.

"Did Telly just muck the card into Fat Bastard East's face?" Stu roared.

Kevin was doubled over, wheezing from laughing so hard. "The balls on this guy!"

The next hand was another win for Telly. An official came over to shake his hand and said, "Follow me."

"Am I getting kicked out?" he asked hopefully. Clutch couldn't blame him if he was expelled for hitting Fat Bastard East in the face with a card. After all, it was

Clutch's fault anyway. Telly turned toward the exit, but the man in the suit grabbed his arm.

"The exit is that way," Telly told him.

"So?" the attendant asked.

"Shouldn't we be heading that way?"

"Please follow me, Mr. Martin." Telly was led into a room with a single table with blazing lights overhead. He heard Clutch sing like an angel. He couldn't see the audience; the uplight blocked it. It was as if the table were on a stage. There was a player sitting with a mountain of chips before him, his eyes watching Telly like a predator.

"Is this…?" Telly asked, his voice barely a whisper.

"Nirvana, heaven, the main table." Clutch was skipping around the table. "I didn't think it could get any better, but it did! Look who made it here too!" He stood behind Adam "the Ant" Antonowski, pointing with both hands at the younger man's head.

"This is our live streaming table, broadcast around the world as the action is happening," said the official. Telly watched as his chips were laid reverently in piles on his corner of the felt.

"You want me to play in front of…"

"Millions and millions of people. Now, gentlemen, if you could please stand behind me, I will lead you in." Seven people stood behind him, cracking knuckles and fussing with hair. There were two women, and the rest were men.

Clutch was dancing around. "This is it, kid. You've arrived."

"I injured another player. What kind of people are you?" Telly asked. *How could this be happening?*

The executive laughed. "Everybody hates Fat Bastard East. You unnerved him, and he lost his next hand. Brilliant strategy." He turned to Telly. "It's like you do what we all want to do but don't have the guts to do. You've become something of a hero."

Telly stepped onto the big stage, Clutch right behind him. He rubbed Telly's shoulders like a prize fighter. Telly shrugged him away. "Ow." Clutch's cold hands hurt.

"Lotta chips, Telly," Oscar, a grizzled meat packer from Chicago, observed.

"Evening, everyone," Telly said. "How did you know my name?" He took a seat and smiled at the rest of the players. Everyone but Ant smiled back.

"Everybody in the poker world knows Telly 'No Tells' Martin. You are supposedly real good at reading everyone." This from Honey Potts, an actress who was chewing on the end of an unlit cigar.

"I don't think so...I have a confession to make," Telly said, his face serious.

The room froze. It was so quiet, you could hear Telly breathing.

"I am not playing alone. I am listening to someone tell me what to do. I have been listening to Clutch Henderson. It's true. Clutch is channeling his energy through me. That's the only reason I'm winning. He's with me right now." Telly felt like a load had been lifted from his shoulders.

There was stunned silence. Oscar rose to his feet as slowly as his big, ponderous body would allow. He raised his thick hands and began clapping, his head bowed toward Telly. "You're a class act, No Tells. That's about the nicest thing I ever heard."

One by one, each player rose, until the room was filled with thunderous and appreciative applause.

From the gallery, a cheer started and soon took over the whole room. "Clutch, Clutch, Clutch!"

Ruby stood, taking Ginny's hand to stand beside her. "Clutch, Clutch, Clutch!" Even Stan joined the crowd.

"No, no, you don't understand." Telly stood, waving his hands for them to stop. The shouting got louder, like a marching army. Clutch beamed.

"Clutch, Clutch, Clutch!"

"I'm listening to him tell me what to do," Telly pleaded to the chanting crowd.

The chant changed, becoming louder. People were clapping their hands in time to the words. "Listen to Clutch! Listen to Clutch!"

In the casino, people stopped playing to join the chant. On the couch, Harriet and Frank raised their arms, shrimp wrapped in bacon in each hand, and yelled, "Listen to Clutch! Listen to Clutch!"

At the Tango Motel, Quick Daddy and Cheryl sat in their living room, holding their hands together and aloft, shouting, "Listen to Clutch! Listen to Clutch! Listen to Clutch!"

At the county jail, the prisoners sat clustered around the TV, their hands chained together, their voices singing, "Clutch, Clutch, Clutch!"

Jenny Henderson covered her ears with both hands to drown out the cries.

Victor Mazzone, who had made bail for Jenny after she signed away most of the inheritance, smiled as he sang, "Clutch, Clutch, Clutch!"

"I could have told you that would happen." Clutch was next to him, smirking. "They love me." He walked out to center stage, his chest pushed out, his arms opened wide, enjoying every second. "They love me. It's Clutchtime!" he shouted. Then he turned to Telly. "Now sit your dumb ass down and let's win this thing. You ain't gettin' rid of me until the fat lady sings, and I don't hear no voices. You're in too deep, and for some stupid reason, they love you too. Go ahead and channel the shit out of me, baby. I'm yours. Oscar has pocket deuces. If you get your head out of your ass, you'll see there's a two on the turn, so… reraise."

Telly reraised.

It was the Ant's turn. Clutch shouted in the younger man's ear. "You suck, bro. The Ant is marching one by one! Knock this twerp out already, Telly."

"I'm all in," Telly said woodenly.

The Ant folded, safe for another game.

"Call," Oscar said. He lost all his chips and was done. He rose, and Telly got up to shake his hand. The Ant stuck his tongue out. Oscar turned around, gave the hooded man the finger, and said, "Clutch, Clutch, Clutch." His fist was raised in the air as he bounced off the stage.

Telly couldn't hear Clutch over the insults hurled by the Ant. Hunched, his hoodie covering his greasy hair, he sneered, his nasty teeth feral in his snarl. "You call me with a five–six offsuit, you twit? Now look at the mess you've gotten into." The Ant was speaking to Honey Potts.

Honey Potts mucked her cards, knowing the game was all over for her. She bluffed and lost. She slapped Telly on the back and said, "Go get him, No Tells. Do it for Clutch." She blew him a kiss as she left the room. "Clutch, Clutch, Clutch" became her swan song too.

Both Telly and the Ant were apparently unstoppable. Just a few more plays, and it was just the two of them.

"It went quickly, Kev," Stu said into the mick. "But not as quickly as me in the bedroom."

"I'll say. Two more to go, and we are in the home-stretch."

The cards were revealed. "Jack high flush." The retired postman smiled. "You've come a long way from the Mirage poker room, Telly. It was a pleasure playing with you. I can now say I played with the greatest player in the game."

"One more, the final roundup. Let's squash this ant," Clutch whispered into Telly's ear.

"Historic, absolutely historic. This is it, folks. The reigning champion versus No Tells. Adam 'the Ant' Antonowski has done it again. He beat nearly twelve thousand players to get here…again." Kevin approached the table to squat down beside the Ant.

"If you bring up the name Clutch or Telly, I walk."

"Let me ask you a question before we go to commercial break, Ant. If you were stranded on a desert island

and had a choice between In-N-Out or Jack in the Box, which would you pick?"

"Is this a trick question?" Ant spat.

"You told me not to bring up Clutch or Telly." Kevin smiled, all his teeth showing.

Somewhat mollified, the Ant thought and then answered, "Two double doubles with onions. One animal-style French fries, and a vanilla shake."

"That's what I thought…right, Stu?" He winked at the other announcer.

"I love a good double shake." They were sharing a joke at his expense, but he be damned if he couldn't figure it out.

"And a good vanilla shake," Kevin persisted.

Stu laughed and then took the cue. "Speaking of vanilla shakes, Telly Martin has shaken up the poker universe with near flawless gameplay."

The Ant threw down a towel he was using. "I hate you guys!" He stormed off, their laughter echoing after him.

Kevin moved to Telly. "So, Telly, where is Clutch right now?"

Telly turned to face him, his expression relaxed. "Right next to me."

"That's simply fascinating," Kevin said, his eyes bright.

"I'm sure it sounds that way," Telly responded.

He pulled over a chair to sit. "What is he telling you right now?"

"You're a turd, Kev," Clutch leaned over and said into the mike. No one heard but Telly.

Telly took the mike and smiled. "He says he really likes you."

Kevin beamed. "Well, I like him too. So, if you win the bracelet, in a way so does Clutch."

"I can't see it any other way," Telly agreed.

"The bracelet is mine!" Clutch stood on the table and beat on his chest.

"Are you nervous about going up against the reigning champion?" the announcer asked.

Indignant, Clutch shouted, "No!"

Telly was thoughtful. "Well…"

"No, no, no!" Clutch insisted.

"No," Telly sighed.

"What's your strategy?"

Telly was silent for a minute. He looked over at Clutch, who was sitting almost on top of him. Clutch's face was serene, blissful. He was having the time of his life. *Oops,* Telly amended. *The time of his death, perhaps.* His dreams appeared close to being fulfilled.

"Listen to Clutch," he said simply.

* * *

"Is this seat taken?" Gretchen asked a bald man, pointing to the seat next to him.

He moved his hat from the cushion. "No, no, it's yours."

"Great," Gretchen smiled.

"Stan Jarvis." Then he added, "This is Ginny and Ruby."

Gretchen held out her hand to each of them. "Pleasure to meet you. Are you enjoying the Series?"

Stan blew air from his lips. "This is the most exciting Series I've been to. I love that guy, Telly. He's a character."

Gretchen smiled. "He's my fiancé."

"Well, I love him!" Stan smiled. "He's some bright guy."

"He's brilliant. He designed the computer network for this casino."

"You don't say! Why is he driving a cab then?"Stan asked.

"How did you know that?" she asked.

"He took me for a ride." Stan chuckled.

"Long story. He's between jobs right now."

"Happens I need a network. Got to link seventy of my restaurants." He pulled out a business card. "Tell him to call my man Howard. If Howard approves, I've got a nice job for him in Phoenix if he wants it."

Gretchen took the card and placed it in her purse. Gretchen was having a good day. A very good day.

* * *

The interview ended, and the announcer was brought in to do the opening. "For the thousands in attendance and the millions watching around the world, ladies and gentlemen, it's time to shuffle up and deaaaal!" Applause and cheers erupted in the gallery. Telly narrowed his eyes but could not see Gretchen. He touched his lips, then his heart, knowing she was doing the same.

"Calm down; just be cool. That little pissant will never know what hit him." Clutch was bouncing from one foot to the other like a demented boxer.

"And now, sitting on the east end of the table…he's the defending champion. He's small, but he can carry his weight in chips. Ladies and gentlemen, Adam 'the Ant' Antonowski!"

Clutch was rubbing his shoulders again. "I told you not to do that!" Telly said.

"Sorry." Clutch leaned close, his cold breath in Telly's ear. "Now listen, he's going to try and get into your head. Don't listen to his smack."

"Gosh, I don't know what that feels like," Telly said sarcastically.

"Oh, you mean me?" Clutch looked innocent. "Just do what I say. No showboating. Don't let him intimidate you."

"Now, fighting out of the west end of the stage… a no-name, newbie local who channels the greats of the past. At the end of a near flawless Series—the one, the only, Telly 'No Tells' Martin!"

Telly walked into the lighted arena; the table was at center stage. He felt the hair on his neck stand up as the heat of the overhead lights scorched his skin. The air in the room was different—weighted and thick. Telly automatically looked to Clutch, who was, well, white as a ghost. His face was frozen in fear, his eyes opened wide, his mouth drawn back in a silent scream. Suddenly, Clutch ran forward, hissing, "Buster, what the fuck are you doing here?"

Telly looked into the abyss on the other side of the room and caught an ominous dark shadow ponderously making its way across the stage. It was oppressive, a hulking presence that sucked the light and air from the room.

Clutch checked himself, his form vibrating with anger. "Holy shit." He turned to Sten, who was calmly leaning against a camera, and demanded, "Did you know he was here?"

Telly heard him. "Sten?" He looked around. There were more of them?

"What's the matter, Clutch? You look like you saw a ghost," Buster said with a laugh. Only Clutch could hear it. He was in hell.

"Get lost, Gramps," Clutch sneered. "This is my game."

"Like hell, Oliver. You don't own the world. You're nothing but a two-bit cheat and card shark."

"Ready, old man?" the Ant asked.

Telly looked at him, perplexed. "I'm not old. Who are you talking to?"

The Ant looked around the stage as if he were listening to directions. "Who are *you* talking to?"

Telly pointed to him slowly. "I'm talking to *you*."

Clutch walked in front of Telly to confront the hulking shadow. "You're helping this little insect?" His voice dripped with anger.

"You bet I am," Buster told him.

Clutch stood for a minute in stunned silence. "You hustled me? The whole tourney, you hustled me? How come I didn't see you?"

"You only see what you want to see, Oliver. That's been your problem all along."

Telly turned to Clutch and whispered, "Who are you talking to?"

The Ant stood, the veins on his neck bulging. "I said I was talking to you!"

"Did you help him win last year, Buster?" Clutch asked.

Telly repeated, "Buster?"

The old man laughed and said, "Oh, Clutch, that was one hell of a game."

The Ant looked at Telly, finally realizing what was going on and said, "Clutch?"

Telly put it together: he could hear Clutch, and the Ant was apparently listening to Buster Henderson, the ghost of Clutch's grandfather.

Kevin jumped out of his seat. "This is unprecedented, folks. In a nod to two of the greatest poker legends in the history of the game, the Ant is calling Telly *Clutch,* and Telly is calling the Ant *Buster,* Clutch's grandfather."

"Wow," Stu said in awe. "This is a change from the disrespect we've seen at the tables lately. Maybe Telly 'No Tells' has brought manners back to the game. This is so special."

Kevin agreed. "This Series will go down in history as a real game changer."

Clutch was so still that Telly could barely see him.

"You told him my hand," Clutch accused.

"Yup," Buster said with no malice, but a hint of sadness.

Telly heard the hurt in Clutch's voice when he asked, "Why did you ruin my game, Grandpa? Why?"

"Oh, Clutch, you still don't get it. After all this time, you don't understand. You never learned the real game. Poker is a game of respect."

"Like you respected me last year?" Clutch stomped forward, his hands fisted.

"You were selfish then, and you are selfish now. All you ever cared about was yourself."

"Well, someone had to!" Clutch yelled. "Nobody else did." He reached out to punch the shadow. Telly watched, aghast, as something drove Clutch to his knees.

On the screens, the anchormen watched as Telly and the Ant simply stared at each other silently, their faces blank. Cards were dealt, and Telly looked at his pocket sevens, waiting to hear what to do. The Ant studied the cards in his hand, his hoodie off, sweat dripping down his forehead.

Buster and Clutch, on the other hand, were duking it out like prizefighters. All the Ant heard was Buster's grunts as he watched his huge body being slammed to the floor.

Telly stared as Clutch rolled across the stage, locked in combat with an unseen foe.

"You piece of shit. How could you do that to me? I'm your blood!" Clutch shouted.

"You're nothing better than cow turd. Lazy care-for-nothing narcissist!" Buster responded hotly.

"Narcissist? Where'd you learn that word? From him, I bet!" He pointed to Sten, who watched impassively.

"All you ever cared about was your own pleasure. Never gave two shits about anyone else—not your kid, not Jenny, not Ginny. Redemption's a bitch," Buster said between punches. "You never worked for or appreciated anything in your life."

"That's a lie!" Clutch was enraged. "You took the bracelet away from me!"

"That's right, boy. That's why I *really* called you Clutch, because you want everything in your greedy clutches."

"I had to be that way. I never had anything, just your leavings. No mother, no father, just you and that old besom, Ruth. You never cared for me. The game was the most important thing in your life. Those were the cards you dealt me."

They were both on the floor, breathing hard. Buster laughed bitterly. "That was the lesson, you dope. Poker is life. The hand you're dealt is determined. It's how you play the cards that counts. Does the circumstances make the person, or does the person make the circumstances?"

Clutch looked up in astonishment. "I was the best poker player in the world."

"None of that mattered when you failed at everything else. It was always up to you, Oliver. You made the wrong choices." Buster sat up and touched Clutch's shoulder gently. "I tried to teach you that in real life, and now in the afterlife too. Look at what you lost by always trying to win."

Clutch placed his hands over his eyes to stop the hot tears that prickled his eyelids. *The wrong choices.* A kaleidoscope of memories cascaded like falling cards—the missed birthdays, the family dinners gone cold while he played, the extramarital affairs, the hurts, the petty fights to get out of his responsibilities. Did he ever tell any of them he loved them?

Clutch sighed and stood up, holding out a hand to help his grandfather. He brushed off his pants. Turning to Telly, he said, "I'm sorry, Telly. What I did was wrong."

Telly watched Clutch, his eyes wide in his face.

"You got integrity," said Clutch. "I know you're gonna do the right thing. You never needed me to tell you what to do."

Telly's eyes smarted with tears, but strangely he felt no panic. He could do this.

"I fold, partner." Clutch winked.

Clutch turned and walked toward a swirling tunnel, his arm over the hulking cloud, finally at peace. He vanished. Sten followed with a satisfied smile, closing the portal behind them.

Telly searched the stage. Clutch was gone. He looked at the Ant, who was scanning the area nervously. Telly shrugged. The Ant shrugged back.

"I guess we're on our own," Telly said quietly to the Ant. He looked down at the three cards on the baize. Ace, two, and four stared back at him, burned into his retina.

The Ant nodded. "Guess so." He gulped, his Adam's apple bobbing in his skinny neck. He looked about twelve years old.

Telly pushed a mountain of chips into the center. "Bet four million."

The Ant looked at his stacks and then up at Telly. Telly noticed he had startling green eyes that were rimmed in red. He had to lean forward to hear the Ant murmur, "I'm all in."

"This is it!" Kevin was breathless. "We're in the first hand, and the Ant's gone all in? If Telly calls…"

"Call," Telly said simply, revealing his two sevens.

The Ant smiled, his crooked teeth showing as he turned over pocket kings.

"Good hand, Adam," Telly smiled. The Ant looked up tentatively, grinning back.

"Here comes the turn," Kevin's voice came over the speakers.

The dealer placed a four next to the other cards. The Ant stood, his knuckles pressed into the table. Telly noticed his face was full of pimples. He couldn't have been older than twenty-two.

Telly took a long look at the audience, wishing he could see Gretchen. He touched his lips, then his heart, knowing she would get the message. He took off his glasses, rubbing his tired eyes. Placing them on again, he said with determination, "Let's get this over with."

The river came with agonizing slowness. The card flipped over to land in the row. Telly stared blankly at the seven of diamonds. The crowd was on its feet, screaming. The Ant looked up at Telly, a sweet smile on his face.

"Nicely played. Congratulations." He held out his freckled hand to shake Telly's.

"Well, that was fun."

"Yeah," the Ant said. "Let's do it again."

Telly nodded. The announcer jumped onto the stage.

"Telly, Telly, you did it! You steamrolled twelve thousand people to defeat your opponent. How did you do it?" Kevin pushed the mike into his stunned face.

"By sticking with it through thick and thin." He scanned the now-lighted room, looking for Gretchen. He held out his hand for her to join him.

"What are you planning to do with your winnings?" Kevin asked.

"After a few expenses and taxes, it's being donated to charity." Gretchen was led up to him, her face relieved. "I couldn't have done it without you," he told her gratefully.

Gretchen smiled. "I think we are having a good day. By the way, I'm pregnant."

Telly smiled. "It's official. I am the luckiest man in the world."

Epilogue

Four Months Later

Gretchen sat in the rented Ford Explorer, Sophie on what was left of her lap. Her pregnancy was in the last part of the fourth month and competed for space with the dog. She had gained a little too much weight. All that CiCi's Pizza was adding up. Telly had helped Cheryl and Earl (formerly known as Quick Daddy) purchase their franchise.

"Well, Mrs. Martin. Are you ready?" Telly took her hand and kissed her knuckles. "I still wish you would have let me buy you that yellow diamond, if only to see that creepy saleslady's face."

"Telly," she gushed, "you're my diamond. I don't want any of that kind of stuff. I'm glad you donated all that money to charity. There are people who really need it. All I need is you."

They had put together a foundation, creating retraining programs for jobless people to go to school and train for new careers. They had set up scholarships in several of the trade schools and colleges, the Culinary Institute of Nevada getting a sizable chunk. Telly loved the irony that Clutch's daughter Ruby was the recipient of the first scholarship.

"The freeway is that way," Gretchen said, pointing to the left. "Where are we going?"

They had just pulled away from his parents' house, saying a tearful good-bye before they proceeded with their move to Phoenix. Telly was going to run the IT department at Stan's Barbeque—the job paid double his former wages at the casino. They had a home and a car waiting for them in Arizona. They had become close with Stan and his new wife, Ginny.

"I have to make a quick stop." Telly drove to Mount of Olives Cemetery in western Vegas. He pulled under a sweeping olive tree, the namesake of the cemetery. "Wait here. I'll be back in a moment."

He walked down four aisles, his hands in his pockets. He found the stone covered by rotted leaves and a few twigs. Telly bent down, clearing away the debris. Ginny had purchased the grave before she'd moved out of Vegas and placed the urn in there. She didn't know what to do with what was left of his cremains once she married Stan. She wanted Ruby to have somewhere to go if she felt alone.

"Thanks for waking me up." Telly smiled when he heard Clutch's snarky voice. "What, no kiss good-bye?"

"I figure you're in the ninth circle of hell by now," Telly said, his eyes misting.

"Naw, not yet. You'll never believe it, but they have great therapists here."

"Really?"

"Yeah, we're working on my commitment issues. So, Phoenix?"

Telly sat on his haunches. "I'm happy with it."

"And poker?"

Telly shook his head. "No fun without you."

"Aw shucks, Telly. You're making me blush."

Telly stood, reaching into his pocket. He pulled out the chunky gold bracelet. "I want to thank you, Clutch. It was amazing."

He could hear Clutch's gasp and feel the emotion as he placed the bracelet on the headstone. Telly stood, shyly wiping his eye.

"Hey, Tel," he heard Clutch call as he walked away, "I heard you're pretty good at craps."

Telly shook his head and laughed. "Don't even think about it."

Author's Note

The International Series of Poker is a fictional tournament, as are all of the characters in the book. It's loosely based on the World Series of Poker, which happens every year in Las Vegas and takes numerous days to complete. In the interest of brevity, I whittled it down to a two-day tournament.

22462743R00152

Made in the USA
Middletown, DE
31 July 2015